KARTER & JAMAR 2

A SPECIAL LOVE AFFAIR

ANAK AND TINA B.

Karter & Jamar 2

Copyright © 2019 by Tina B. & Anak

Published by Shan Presents
www.shanpresents.com

All rights reserved. No part of this book may be used or reproduced in any form or by any means electronic or mechanical, including photocopying, recording, or by information storage and retrieval system, without the written permission from the publisher and writer, except brief quotes used in reviews.

This is a work of fiction. Any references or similarities to actual events, real people, living or dead, or to the real locals intended to give the novel a sense of reality. Any similarity in other names, characters, places, and incidents are entirely coincidental.

SUBSCRIBE

Text Shan to 22828 to stay up to date with new releases, sneak peeks, contest, and more....

SUBMISSIONS

To submit your manuscript to Shan Presents, please send
the first three chapters and synopsis
to submissions@shanpresents.com

1

KARTER

"I have Karson's bag. Can you just get the girls' shoes on?" Jamar asked me.

I smiled and fixed his buttons to his button down shirt. Today was a big day, and I couldn't even hide the excitement. Jamar was rocking a white Balmain shirt with some matching white Balmain jeans. On his feet was some all-white Yeezys that I picked out. Since Jamar's rank moved up in the streets he became flashy as hell. He kept his jewelry on ice berg. I mean his jewelry game was so icy. I didn't mind, though. My man deserved to show what he worked hard for!

Jamar's dreads were freshly retwisted pulled up into four braids to the back. It was a white affair so I made sure the whole family of attendance was rocking white. White was kind of the family signature color when we stepped out. I walked into Mariel's room and she was struggling to put her stockings on.

"Mommy can you help me?" Mariel cried. I pulled her stockings on, and she slipped her feet into her all white dress shoes. I made sure Mariel and Jamie, my five-year-old daughter, had the same hairstyle and dress. We always dressed them like twins, which of course they loved too.

"Okay, go downstairs and tell ya daddy to take y'all pictures." I told them and they ran off after I fixed the ribbons in their hair. I had literally one hour to get to the venue where the ceremony was being held at. I went to my room and took my robe off. I oiled my body down with my coconut oil and slipped on my under clothes. I stepped in my white Vera Wang fitted pants one-piece.

It was fitted tightly to my shape, and on my feet, I went with some Chanel heels that strap around the ankles. I had my new Chanel Side Pack Quilted White Lambskin Leather Cross Body Bag on my arm. I made sure my gun was tucked inside my purse and grabbed all my other accessories. Looking at myself in the mirror, my makeup was beat to the gods, and CiCi snapped on my thirty-two inch frontal. I was popping, and my family looked just as good.

"You look beautiful wife." Jamar smirked and kissed my lips.

"Thanks daddy." I laughed, and he looked at his watch.

"Come on ma. The security here." He said and grabbed Karson. I grabbed the bag and ushered the kids out the door.

We got twenty minutes to be there. I hope everybody else is set." I told Jamar going through my missed emails, texts, and calls. I had a few missed calls from private numbers but I deleted them and put my phone in my purse. I made a mental note to get my number changed as soon as possible.

Today is going to be a good day.

"KARTER TAYLOR." The dean called my name to get my

Master's Degree. I was finally done with college with my Master's in Clinical Psychology degree. I was ready for my life to begin.

Pow. Pow. Pow.

Dropping to the floor for cover was my first instinct, but then I remembered my children was in the same building. I reached for my gun that I had in my purse and held it close to me as I ran back to where my family was sitting. Everybody was running and diving as gun fire steady erupted in and outside of the building.

"Jamar!" I yelled and nobody called back to me. The closest exit door I saw I headed towards it and people were running out the same door. When I got outside I saw Jamar's security ushering my children into Jamar's bulletproof truck. I sighed and ran towards them. I couldn't tell who was shooting because the security Jamar hired was on it! I hopped into the passenger seat and the driver pulled off. I started to count my kids.

"One, two, three..." I started to count off.

"We all here mommy." Mariel yelled out and I sighed.

"Are y'all okay? Is everyone okay?" I asked unbuckling and taking Karson out the car seat looking him over.

"Yes Mrs. Karter, everyone is okay. We have the rest of the family right behind us." The driver Deno spoke. I sighed and leaned back.

"This some bullshit!" I mumbled and looked at my kids. They were all playing on they tablets in they own worlds like we weren't just in a shoot-out five minutes before.

Ring. Ring. Ring.

"Hello?" I answered.

"Next time we won't miss!" The caller said and hung up. Chills ran through my body as I quickly looked through the mirrors and behind us.

"Jamar is in the car behind us right?" I asked Deno.

"Yes ma'am." I sat back and deleted the blocked call. I guess I was gone have to tell Jamar about this. Unbeknownst to him, I was getting these phone calls for about six months now. At first it was just calling and hanging up. Then it was following me or Jamar. Now it was this.

"Fuck!" I said lowly under my breath. I dialed a number and waited until the caller answered.

"Hello?" Mace answered.

"Hey bro?"

"What's up sis? Long time no hear." He said and I smiled. After both my brothers moved out they never moved back. They both went to college, and now Mason is a P.I. and one of the best in the states. Mace works for Jamar's Organization being their technology engineer.

"I need a huge favor. That stays between me and you." I told him and he sighed.

"What you do?" he asked, and I laughed to lighten the mood.

"Screen my calls. The next private call I get, pin the location for me." I told him, and he typed away on his computer, I assumed.

"Sis, what's up? What happened?" I sighed and looked at my kids. Starting to get emotional, I blew a breath out. "Someone shot up my ceremony. I had the kids with me...." I said.

"We on our way!" Mace snapped and hung up before I could even object. I put the phone down and looked at Deno.

"How's Ana?" I asked, and he smiled big as hell.

"She's doing good man. She getting ready to graduate also next week." He told me and smiled genuinely.

"That's good. I gotta send my girl something. I'm proud

of her." I told Deno, and he turned into Eva's compound. A few months after we killed Marlon and Selena, Jamar started to get heavier in the streets. It's been years since we got rid of them, and I'm not understanding why they family wanted revenge so bad now. Jamar finally moved his mother into her own little city. She had her estate locked down like the White House. Jamar wasn't having it no other way either. To be honest that's how all our cribs was since he decided he wanted to take over. We had to be more low-key. When we pulled up we waited until Jamar came to the car. He opened Kartier's door first and hugged KJ. He did the same for each of our kids and came to my side hugging and kissing me. We have four children together now. Kartier and Mariel was the same age, eight. Jamie was six, and Karson, he was ten months.

"You alright?" he asked and I nodded.

"We need to talk. As soon as we can." I told him and he nodded taking Karson out my arms. I followed my kids inside while Jamar's team and the rest of our family followed us inside.

"I need a drink. Come on kids.... Let's eat." Eva said and my mother and all the kids followed her.

Knock. Knock. Knock.

I grabbed my pistol out my back and held it up aiming towards the door because I wasn't taking no chances. Over the past years Jamar and I have been together, Jamar installed in me to shoot first and never ask questions. When he opened the door, Deno and Marcel walked in. Deno and Marcel joined the family maybe a year ago. They both was one of Jamar's men that I trusted other than the immediate family.

"Nobody was left, nobody was hurt." Marcel said and sat down in a chair. Jamar nodded and paced the floor. Everything had calmed down for all of us over the last eight years. Taking Marlon out was the best thing we could have done. Our life was peaceful and we loved it that way which is why I don't understand why all of a sudden shit was starting back up causing problems that we didn't need.

"Mace and Mason on their way here." I said and Jamar looked at me.

"I'mma be the first one to speak up because no one else is saying anything. We gotta find out who the fuck that was!" Kris said and I agreed.

"I don't know if that shit was for us! I mean we ain't had beef in years. Didn't y'all take care of that?" Tiera said and looked at Jamar.

"Well somebody has been calling me private for the last six months." I said lowly. Jamar snapped his neck my way.

"What you just say?" He asked and I sighed.

"I didn't want to say anything because you have been doing so good and haven't nothing came to our door." I ramble but I was cut off.

"Are you serious Karter?" Kris yelled standing up.

"When we left the ceremony somebody called and said next time we won't miss." I told them and the room groaned.

"Man." Jamar said and walked off slamming the door. I guess these last few years was laid back time; now it was pay back.

....

"Mommy can we stay a night please?" Jamie asked tugging at my hand.

"Maw maw said we can stay!" Mariel said also pulling

my other hand. When I looked into Mariel's face, I saw flashbacks of me taking her mother's life. I never told anyone, not even Jamar, but I regretted it certainly. Over the past few years, I have grown to love Mariel like my own. Looking into her beautiful face, one day she would find out I took her real mother away. That's why I regret doing so. When I first killed Selena, I was relieved. Then when I took Mariel in, all the regret came rushing in. If it came down to it, I don't think I would be able to do it all over again.

"Mommy, can we please?" Mariel said and I looked at Jamar.

"Ask daddy." I said and he mugged me. Jamar was in his feelings deeply because I haven't told him about the private calls. Shit, could you blame me? We have been having problems since we got together; I wanted peace. He couldn't blame me for holding out the information.

"Daddy, Maw Maw said we can stay. Can we stay please?" Jamie asked, and Jamar picked both of them up.

"Yes y'all can stay." he said. Both the girls hugged him tightly, got down and ran off. After all the family left, I put the kids to sleep and Jamar and I left. When I had Jamie, Jamar moved us into our own house a little bit outside of the city in a secluded area.

"Bae?" I tried to say but he put his hands up.

"All this shit could've been prevented Kar." He yelled and I looked at him. In the eight years Jamar and I had been together, I can count on one hand how many times he raised his voice. Jamar was perfect to me and for me. You know it's only three perfect men in the world. Papoose, Russell Wilson and Obama of course. Jamar though? Jamar was in his own league. Thugged out like Papoose, sweet and charming like Russel and King fitted like Obama. My nigga was perfect. His love for me was out of this world and we barely even argued. So for Jamar to even be mad and raise his voice at me, I knew I had screwed up royally. Besides, he had me so spoiled that any time he raised his voice I cried.

"Anything could've happened! Right now I'm pissed cause a muthafucka tried me while my seeds was with us!" He yelled.

"Okay, I understand that. You being angry with me isn't gonna get us closer to them!" I tried to reason.

"Man if you would have told me muthafuckas was playing on yo phone, I could've been got to the bottom of it!" Jamar yelled. We pulled up to the gate of our crib. Jamar nodded at the security and he let us through.

"You know we have been trying to get this organization passed down. That's why I have been heavy in the streets. With this shit going on, I'mma be going harder!" He said pulling in the garage. When we let the garage down, the impact of an explosion on our guard tower blew us off our feet. We felt the house shake under us and watched as our security shack burned to ashes. I guess this is the best way to get Jamar and the Black Guerrilla Family out of retirement.

2

JAMAR

"FUCK KARTER!" I snapped.

I wasn't trying to take my anger out on her but *FUCK!* It was hard not to. At age twenty-eight, I'm supposed to be preparing myself for retirement. Shit kept popping up and making me go back to the old me.

"You alright shorty?" I asked helping her off the ground. She had a few minor bruises and cuts.

"I'm good. Are you?" She asked looking over me. I nodded and looked around to make sure nothing was out of the ordinary. The security tower was up in flames, and I could hear the fire trucks getting close.

"Get back in the car Karter." I told her as I got ready to open the garage door that lead to the house.

"Wait, Jamar. Just don't go in yet." She told me and I hesitated.

"Let's just go to yo moms and get the kids." She told me, and I saw the fear on her face. I pulled her into my chest and she hugged me.

"It's gonna be okay! Motherfuckas gotta die for coming

to my crib with this shit." I told her straight up, and that's when the police and firefighters pulled up.

After getting the fire together, I dropped Karter off at my duke's crib and hit the streets. I don't even beat the block no more, but I had to get out here and see what's the word. I know if it was some little niggas they was gone be running they mouth about it. Either way whoever it was, was just as good as dead! Pulling up to my old neighborhood the hood was live. Soon as my feet hit the pavement, my crew was showing love. I saw the neighborhood news anchor Dewayne walking with a group of girls.

"Aye Wayne." I called him and he stopped. He said something to his friends and came walking to me.

"What's up Jamar?" He asked and I smirked.

"I got a good fifty if you can tell me who had something to do with my family getting shot at." I told him and he sighed.

"FIFTY DOLLARS?" He said. "First off all, it's Tete to you! Second of all, I'mma need a little bit more than fifty dollars. Yup the streets been talking! So you said a hundred?" He said and I nodded.

"I got you." I told him.

"Well, word is you fucked with the wrong people. Y'all got Asians, Mexicans, Jamaicans, all type of (Ans) on y'all ass!" He said and I nodded. "I don't got names right now, but I can get some later on tonight!" He told me, and I walked away without paying him. He started calling my name, but I hopped into my car and headed back to my duke's crib. I don't know what's going on, but I was getting answers soon!

3

JANIA

Four years earlier.
"Just leave me alone. I'm calling the police!" I yelled through my door.

I grabbed my son Tyree Jr and put my finger over my lips. I handed him my phone and dialed 9-1-1. Tyree Jr. had tears running down his face, and I prayed Little came home sooner. Kissing my son lips, I shut the closet door and ran to the front room where Jason, my ex-boyfriend, was banging on the door. Jason and I haven't been together for the past five years, and here I am with somebody else, starting a family with somebody else.

"The police on the way." I yelled as I backed up against the wall.

"Bitch, I don't give a fuck about the police!" Jason yelled getting into my face wrapping his hands around my throat.

I scratched at his hand because I couldn't breathe, but he didn't budge. Raising me off my feet, I started to kick. I started to feel light-headed and knew this was the end for me I started to pray for God to forgive me for all my wrongdoings and sins. Then the devil flashed in front of my face.

"You think you can move on with somebody else. Huh?" Jason

roared and threw me against the nearest wall. I gasped for air but couldn't catch it quick enough. He had kicked me in the side causing my whole body to collapse.

"Please.... JUST GO!" I cried out.

Jason grabbed my hair dragging me into the back. I kicked and screamed but my cries fell on death ears.

"Jason. Please stop. I'm sorry." I yelled and he dropped my body.

"You not sorry yet bitch!" He said and started to hit me all over with face and back shots. Wherever and anywhere his fist landed. I felt a crack in my nose then blood started to gush out. The final blow took me out when I saw his foot come crashing down on my face.

BEEP. Beep. Beep.

I JUMPED out my sleep when I heard the noise realizing that my dream wasn't just a dream. It was a nightmare. I noticed I was in a hospital room. Something was in my mouth and nose breathing for me. I tried to pull it out but felt a hand stopping me. Karter was staring at me with tears running down her face.

"You okay?" She asked smiling through her tears.

"Little get up." She yelled, and Tyree jumped up with his pistol in his hand looking around.

"WHAT?" he started to say until he realized I was awake. "I'm gonna get the nurse." He said and rushed out. After a few seconds the doctors rushed in.

"Hello Jania. I'm Nurse Jackie. I have been taking care of you for the past three weeks. You gave us a fright yeah?" She said and I looked at her.

"You're going to feel a little bit of discomfort. I'm going to remove these." She spoke and I nodded my head yeah. After about three minutes, the tubes and breathing machine was out but my mouth still wasn't opening. I touched and felt wires in my mouth and face. I looked at Karter and she looked away.

"Well we couldn't talk about what's going on to them. It's our policy and we don't know the relationship between you all. Is it okay to discuss your condition?" Nurse Jackie asked and I nodded slowly.

"Your jaw was dislocated. We had to wire it shut. You also lost thirteen teeth, you suffered from a broken nose, broken arm in two places, broken leg in two places and a miscarriage." she looked at me with sympathy. I looked at Little because I know if I was pregnant, it was for sure his. We only had sex about four times these past few months because shit been rocky. I haven't been with nobody else in years though.

"You were about... I say five weeks. You may have not known." she spoke and I sighed. The tears started and I couldn't stop them either. "We're gonna get the doctor back. I'm pretty sure you'll be able to leave in about three days." She told me and touched my arm. I nodded and she walked away. Once all the doctors was out the room Little sat on the side of me and pulled me into his arms.

"You good ma!" he said. "Did you know you were pregnant?" He asked. I shook my head no and he sighed. "T-Two at my house with the kids. He was pretty scared sis!" Karter said, and I couldn't even do nothing but cry. I was thankful that Jason didn't know my son was there or it would've turned out worse.

"What's his name?" he asked and I looked at him.

"Nigga she can't talk." Kris said walking into the room. We both laughed at her lightening up the mood. She handed me a bag with a dry erase board and marker inside and she winked at me.

"I'm glad you up sis." Kris spoke and kissed my forehead. After that, everybody else started to come into the room slowly.

The entire time Little stayed by my side. Ever since our first date a few months ago we have been joined at the hip. I know him being so clingy was because he was trying to get over his baby mama. I just kept praying that me going thru this wouldn't push him away.

"Are you iight?" He asked pulling me out of my thoughts. I tried to smile as best as I could. "You still gorgeous." He reassured me then kissed my forehead.

I wrote "Thank you" on the white board.

"Okay sis. Jamar is calling me talking about come get the kids. I'll let you guys have alone time, and I will be back first thing in the morning." Karter said and hugged me tightly.

I wrote on the board, "I love you and thanks."

Karter hugged Little then said her goodbyes and left. "Are you alright? You need anything?" Little asked standing up.

My heart dropped when he stood up. I just knew he was getting ready to leave.

I quickly wrote on the board, "Don't leave me here please".

He sighed and sat back down next to me. "I'm not going nowhere. When you can finally leave you coming home with me. At least until I find that bitch ass nigga." he said, and I let out the breath I was desperately holding.

"I don't want you to get into my beef. Just let it go." I wrote on the board and his neck snapped to look into my face.

"Shorty, you gotta get up and look at yo face. No matter what you say dat nigga dead G! He pulled some weak ass shit while my son was there! YOU NOT SAVING HIM DIS TIME SHORTY," he said ending the conversation.

I sighed and leaned back. I wasn't trying to protect Jason at all. I know Jason, though, and I know what he's capable of. I don't know if it was love that I was feeling for Little, but I know I didn't want him to get hurt because of me.

"Just don't worry about me shorty. I can handle myself." Little told me and stood up again. He went to the bathroom.

Knock. Knock. Knock.

The doctor came into the room.

"Hey Miss Jania Wills. I'm Doctor Kingsley. I have been your doctor since you been here. We were waiting until you woke up. All your injuries are basically going to heal on their own. I have you set for an appointment in seven days then six weeks after that. I have some prescriptions here for you to get in case of pain." He said as Little came out of the bathroom.

"Nah Doc. She good on those. She won't need no pain meds or none of that shit." When he said that I looked at him crazy. I held my hand up to stop Little from talking and started to mumble.

"NOO! I need them. I'm in pain now." I wrote on the board.

"I don't want you to get hooked on them." He said and gave me a look. I sighed and sat there contemplating. I know he was saying that to help me, but I was in pain badly.

Addiction for pills ran deeply in my blood. My mother got hooked on pain meds when she was a teenager and shortly after that turned into crack. Now she's a full blown crackhead on meth. I never told nobody about my mother though except Little. Being ashamed was the main reason. My mother sold me for heroine when I was ten, which caused me to get raped multiple times. She sold me to her pimp at thirteen, where I was forced to turn tricks, and that's how I met Jason. My life went from worst to living in hell on earth.

I felt Little's arms wrap around my body and didn't even realize the doctor was no longer standing in front of me, but I was silently crying. I had demons of my own that I was trying so hard to fight on a daily basis. I was tired of fighting! Since I could remember, I had been getting used and abused. My own mother *didn't protect me. Then the one person that I thought saved me turned out to be the devil.*

"Shawty, you gon be good. I got you." Little said, and with those three words I fell in love with him.

PRESENT

"Get up dada. Get up." I baby talked as I watched my son take a few steps then fall.

"Mommy, where is my daddy?" Tyree Jr asked, and I sighed.

"He should be pulling up." I responded.

Ever since Little and I got married a few years ago, this has been my routine. I'm at home all the time with our sons while he's running the streets. I know him and Jamar was supposedly transitioning to getting out the game forever, but damn, I didn't know the hours putting in the work was gone be longer. Don't get me wrong, I love mommy and wife life, but I needed a well-needed "me" day and I want to spend time with my husband.

"Come on T-two, so y'all can get ready for nap time." I told Tyree Jr.

He pouted and stomped his feet until we got to his room that he shared with Ty when they took naps. My sons were Tyree Jr and Ty. T-two, which everybody called Tyree Jr., is six going on thirty and Ty is only eleven months. Both my sons look just like they damn daddy! They all triplets, and let's not forget about Ty'aira. Shit they quads. I put Ty in his crib and slipped the bars up. I cut the lights off and shut the door. It was going on twelve-thirty in the afternoon, and Little hasn't even been home yet. He didn't come home last night, and I was frustrated as hell. I dialed Karter's number while I straightened up my house.

"Hello?" she answered on the last ring.

"Hey boo, you busy?" I asked and she sighed.

"Girl getting these damn kids down for a nap. Remind me to get my fucking tubes tied!" She groaned.

"Hell naw man." I heard Jamar say and we both laughed.

"Girl boo. That nigga said he wanted twelve kids. That's what you gonna give him." I told Karter and she smacked her lips.

"Yeah okay. Everything after Karson is abort mission period!" She said and I giggled.

"Girl, I was calling to see if Jamar came home last night. Of course he did, because he's there." I said and wondered why Little ain't walked in the door yet.

"Girl yes, he got here maybe ten last night. Little not there?" she asked and I sighed.

"Nope." the phone got quiet on her end, and I heard mumbling, which only answered my next question.

"He's fucking with her ain't he?" I asked knowing the answer.

"I'm not sure. You my girl and all but she doesn't tell me anything that goes on with her and him because she knows you my bestie." Karter said, and I believed her for the most part.

"I gotta go." I sighed and disconnected the call. I dialed my next door neighbor's number and asked could she come sit with the kids for a while. Once she got there I headed out.

I contemplated on turning around so many times on my way to my destination. I didn't know what I would do if I found them together! Little never ever gave me indication that he was cheating on me, but I learned a long time ago don't even go looking!

My stomach dropped when I pulled up to Tiera Condo, and Little's car was parked right next to hers. I sighed and parked next to his. I got out and slowly crept to her door. I was getting ready to knock but stopped when I heard a muffled sound.

"You said you wasn't gone do this no more!" she yelled.

"I'm not! I can't just leave my seeds like that! " Little yelled back.

"What about us? What about yo kids here? We need you here." she yelled back.

"You married ain't you?" he asked and it went silent.

"You are too! Tell me you don't want me to stay with him and I'll divorce him." she said and my stomach dropped.

"I'm sorry T. You know I love you dearly. I can't keep doing Jania like that! She loves me. I can't keep coming over here staying a night fucking you man. This ain't right." he said, and I felt the tears starting to come.

"Well, how she gone feel when she find out I'm carrying yo seed for the third time, and I'm keeping this one!" she boasted.

"Nah shorty. Get rid of it. Tell yo momma I'm on my way to get Ty'aira." he said and the door flung open. All our eyes met, and I could've sworn I saw a little bit of sympathy on Tiera's face. That was quickly replaced with a smirk.

"You want him so bad? You can have him." I simply said taking my ring off and throwing it her way. I took off walking while Little came rushing behind me trying to plead his case. Nothing he said mattered though. We was done and that was final.

4
CHARLES

I sat in my car as I watched my boyfriend of four years hug and kiss a woman. He picked a little girl up, who looked like she was no older than two and hugged her tightly. Glancing harder, I knew she was his daughter; she looked just like his ass! I sighed and dialed his number. Lance put the girl down, grabbed his phone, and looked at it. He looked around the park and slipped his phone back into his pocket.

After the little girl ran off, Lance sat down on the nearest bench and pulled the woman down on his lap. They sat all cozy like that while she laughed at something he whispered in her ear. I dialed his number again, this time he didn't even look at the phone. I punched the steering wheel and started to back out until I saw the woman get up waving her arms in the air. Lance stood up getting into her face. They were arguing about the phone calls he was ignoring making me smile. She slapped him across his face and he called out to his daughter. He hugged and kissed her and walked away. Once he got into his car, my phone started to ring. I ignored it and when he backed out of the parking spot he started to blow my line down until I finally answered.

"What nigga? Don't call me back now!" I said answering the phone.

"Man, where the hell you at? Why you ain't answering?" he asked, and I rolled my eyes feeling so disgusted. I was sick and tired of these down low ass niggas.

"The same place you at! " I replied back fucking with him.

"Yeah couldn't be. I just left the gym. I'm bout to slide." He said.

"Nah, not right now. I'm busy. I'll call you later." I said hanging up before he could answer questions.

When I looked up his Baby mama was standing at my window, the little girl holding her hand. I sighed and rolled my window down.

"How can I help you?" I asked.

"Are you messing with Lance?" she asked.

"And who are you?" I replied back.

"The one you been watching for the last thirty minutes. I peeped you pull up right after him and dialing his number every time his phone ring. Look, Lance and I are married, have been for twelve years since we were eighteen. I'm not sure how long you guys have been doing this little thing but you're not the first MAN. I've known him to mess with a lot, and I'm pretty sure you aren't going to be the last. He doesn't know that I know he's bi-sexual. I do though and have known for many years. Now ,I'm not sure if you know, but he's married and we have four children together," she said and I looked at this bitch like she was crazy.

"Crack? It's crack isn't it?" I asked and she looked at me clueless. "It gotta be crack that you're on for you to tell me all this and you're fine with it!" I said and she looked around.

"So how old is that nigga?" I asked baffled....

"He's 30." she said and looked at me.

"I didn't know he was married let alone 30 with children. That nigga lied about his whole life." I told her straight up.

"That's what he does! He lies." She said and my phone rang. It was him.

"Look, I'm just gone go 'head on and block him. I'mma let y'all have this weird shit." I told her and rolled my window up. She stood there for a second just looking. I ignored her ass and shifted my gear, getting far away from her ass.

Ring. Ring. Ring.

"Hello? What it do fool?" I answered my phone for Jamar.

"Shit, meet us at the spot." he said and I hung up. I did a U-turn and headed to our meet up spot. When I got there the whole crew was there. I was the last to arrive.

"Thanks for joining us." Jamar spoke and I sat down. "I don't know who sent that hit out but somebody is fucking with my family life now. Somebody was bold enough to try me with my seeds and came to my front door with it. I'mma private ass nigga with a private ass life. Don't many know where my family lay their head at. So what I'm saying is either these niggas that's aiming for me plugged in or somebody in this room an opp nigga." He said and stood up.

I pulled my pistol out my pants and cocked it back. I already knew what time it was. I just hope I don't have to body nobody yet. Everybody that was in attendance was the closest we had to family. It was gone hurt me to take out one of my own, but if they was a snake they had to go.

"Boss?" Don, a little nigga that had been working under Brandon, spoke up.

"I'm not sure who the snake is... I know that nigga Rico been asking weird ass questions. I mean every time he came to me wanting to know anything I shut shit down, but I can't speak for anybody else." Don spoke and Jamar nodded.

"Right on little homie." Jamar said.

" I been hearing around town is that you.... Lil Bone been talking to the Jakes?" Jamar said and Bone stood up trying to run to the door. I shot 'em dropping his ass where he stood.

"From here on out, you see any suspicious acting, body it. I don't give a fuck who it is! Anybody step out of line, body em. If ya hear anything in the streets let me know! All I need is a name... A half of a name, face ,something! Play time over!" he said and stood up. All the other niggas scattered. His clean-up crew came and discarded the body of the snitch. Little Brandon, myself, Jamar, and Jamar two niggas, Marcel and Deno, went out to the back.

"Look, what I heard was y'all took one of theirs so they trying to take all of y'all. I'm not sure who it is but they are not from here." Marcel spoke and looked at Jamar.

"It's been some new heads popping up at the clubs. Just find out who they are and who sent them for me.... Tonight we are celebrating. Everybody come out; call the family and tell them to come out. I'm pretty sure if muthafuckas want to see us they gone come join us tonight." Jamar said and I nodded. He was on to something.

When I finally entered my crib, it was going on ten o'clock. Lance was laying on the couch typing on his phone.

"I have been calling you all day. What's up with you?" he

asked and pulled me down on his lap. Everything in me wanted to attack but I held my composure. I wanted so badly to flash out but I couldn't. Over the years, Lance and I shared so many memories and love. I can't even believe he was playing me the whole time.

"You don't never not answer the phone for me. What's with you?" he said and I stood up.

"Look, I'm not feeling well. I gotta get out and do some shit. So I'll see you tomorrow." I told him walking to the back.

I was beyond pissed. When I got in the shower, I couldn't get my mind off Lance and his ugly ass wife. Every nigga I got with played me to the left and, at this point, I was done giving niggas my time. After I got dressed, I headed out. I was wearing some fitted Balmain jeans with zippers down the legs, with a white silk Versace shirt. On my feet was some white Versace loafers with gold trimmings around. Of course, I had my jewelry on.

When I pulled up to Head Huncho, I made sure I was strapped up and walked straight thru. Ever since Jamar and Brandon opened this club up last year, it's been doing great! It was packed as fuck so I scoped the scene out, looking for any enemies, then headed to the VIP where my niggas was. First, I saw Jamar and Karter. They was boo'd up, and I instantly started to miss Lance. Him being married with a wife bothered me deeply. He lied and told me he was from out of town and didn't have no family here.

A few years back, his brother got killed and he had to go back to his hometown for the funeral. I never met none of his family but he met all mine. Not once has he ever brought up children or a wife. Come to think about it, we been messing around for the last six years, and he hasn't asked me to marry him. He played me big time, and even after all that I still loved him deeply. Lance really the only serious relationship that lasted years, with no problems! None of my relationships worked out, and I gave my love to all the wrong niggas in the past.

In the streets, I would've killed niggas for less, but when it come to this love shit, I let niggas run all over me. Jamar and Brandon hated that shit too. They used to beat all the neighborhood under-covers up for playing me. It was my karma, though. I done killed so many niggas. I guess God said when you done killing, I'll send you somebody that's worth loving you.

"What's up bitch?" Kris yelled hugging me.

This bitch was a drunk. Ever since she had that last baby a few months ago she had been drinking a lot. Too much for me but to each his own.

"Hey hoe. " I greeted everyone else. I glanced around the club and nothing seemed out of place.

After a while of mingling and partying, I started feeling something was about to pop off. Jamar was looking around so he must've felt the vibes, too. My eyes landed on somebody at the bar. He wasn't drinking but he kept whispering to the bartender then they would look up here. He looked so familiar, but I couldn't remember where I knew him from.

"Who is that?" I asked Little and he looked at me.

"That's uh Jamaican cat from up north." Little said and my antennas went up.

"Jamaican? Wasn't-"

Before I could even finish my thoughts gunshots rang out. I pulled my piece out aiming for whoever was shooting.

"Fuck!!" I heard Tiera husband Markel yell out. I saw one shooter and shot to his legs. The club started to clear with everybody running and dodging bullets. When the gunfire ended and the smoke cleared three other people were laid out.

"Help me get her up man. She pregnant!" Little yelled out. When those words came out it was like everybody stopped for a second then jumped back into motion. Markel picked her up and carried her outside.

"Grab that nigga.... Call the ambulance." I yelled to Marcel and Deno. The manager of the club dialed the police and we got out of there following Little to the hospital. I prayed little sis wasn't fucked up the whole way or niggas was gone feel it.

5

JAMAR

"Fuck, Fuck, FUCK!. Gooo, drive this muthafucka!" I yelled hitting the back of the seat.

"Te.... you gone be okay." I whispered trying to calm Tiera down. She was panicking and trying to move.

"Don't let my baby die Jamar. Please." she cried and I sighed.

"It's Tyree's baby. Make sure my baby make it." she cried more and the tears I was trying to hold fell down.

"You got this sis. You and the baby gone be straight. It's just a graze." Karter said rubbing Tiera's head.

"You gone be okay. We almost to the hospital." Karter said kissing her forehead.

"I don't think we gone make it," Tiera said and Little looked back from the driver's seat making us swerve.

"DRIVE THIS BITCH!" I yelled and he stepped on the accelerator.

"Jamar, I don't think I'mma...." Tiera's body started to shake and her eyes rolled into the back of her head.

"Sis... Please sis......" I cried like a baby trying to get her to stay with us.

"We here, we here. Sis, we is here." Karter yelled and opened the door before the car came to a complete stop.

"We need a Doctor. Aye, we need a Doctor." I heard Karter yell and everything went black.

....

"Who the fuck is you?" Karter yelled.

"I'm Ashley Cain. Uh, you must be Karter. Jamar's wife." I heard another familiar voice.

"Yes. I'm his wife and mother of his four children. Who are you again?" Karter replied this time with more attitude.

"I'm Ashley. I go by A.C... I was Jamar's C.O when he was locked down a few years back." Ashley said and all my memories with her came flooding back making my eyes pop open. I was in the hospital room fully dressed but my arm was bandaged up.

"Fuck!" I growled when I leaned on my arm.

"Baby, you awake. You was shot in the arm through and through. You didn't even know though. The doctors said it could've been shock that made you pass out." Karter said kissing my lips.

"Look I don't want no trouble. I just came here to get a swab." Ashley said, and I felt Karter body tense up under my touch.

"What you mean swab?" Karter asked, and that's when I noticed a little girl that looked about nine years old.... She was my spitting image. Or should I say Jamie's spitting image. She looked like she could be Jamie's twin.

"Man fuck!" I yelled getting up.

"Look, I been looking for you and you are hard to find. I

went by the club last night, but it was taped off. Then I heard your sister got shot. So we came up here, so I could see if I could get a swab. I'm married and my husband tested my daughter. He wasn't the father and you the only person I slipped up with." Ashley said looking at me and then Karter. I can see the hurt on Karter's face and I expected nothing less. She was witnessing the man of her life talking to other women about a child that he might could have fathered.

"Yes, I'm pretty sure we could get the test done right quick." Karter spoke up and left out the room. She wasn't gone for no time before she came back in with an older lady.

"This is nurse Kelly. She's gonna do the test for a small fee." Karter said and went fishing in her purse. She handed the lady a rubber band wrapped in 20s. The lady swabbed me then the little girl. I didn't need a DNA though. Little mama looked just like me.

"I'll be back in six hours with the results." The nurse spoke and Karter sighed.

"I mean four," she changed and walked out.

"Until then, give me and my husband some alone time." Karter said and walked out of the room with my hand in hers.

"We need to talk now!" she scolded and walked away down the hall. She entered the room and my whole family was in there surrounding Tiera's bed. Tiera was asleep and the room was filled with a beating sound.

"She's okay. The baby is okay." Little said and Markel huffed and stood up. He bumped past Little and sat his ring down on the table and left out.

Makel was a great dude for Teira. She fucked it up though messing around with Little.

"She was shot twice in the legs, once in the back and it came out the side." Kris said and rubbed Tiera's hand.

"She strong as fuck. The doctor said she was surprised the baby is okay with all the trauma." Little said and sat down.

"Nigga, go home to yo wife!" Kris said and we all chuckled except Karter. She was in her own thoughts sitting by my mother. My mother hadn't said a word either since I walked in.

"Ma." she held her hand up to silence me.

"I never say anything when it comes to you and your life. I have always been your biggest supporter. This time, Jamar, it hit too close. I thought you getting shot was a wakeup call... I'm sick of it. You gotta get out Jamar." My mother pleaded with tears running down her face. My heart broke into pieces just looking into her eyes.

IF YOU KNOW MADUKES, you know she was playful and raw as hell. Crying and begging was never my momma.

"I'mma handle it ma! I promise." I told her and she sighed and didn't say anything else. Karter mugged me and stood up. She walked out and I followed her. When we got outside of the hospital she finally stopped walking.

"Are you gonna talk?" she asked and I sighed.

"Look shorty, A.C. was way before you even was thought of. I mean, if that's my seed I'm gone step up and take care of her. No doubt.... but that's it. I mean, I don't want it to be. I want all my kids by you." I told her pulling her against me.

"I'm telling you now. If she yours and if I feel like that bitch on any type of bullshit I'mma body her ass." Karter said and smiled.

"We good?" I asked her and she kissed my lips.

"Always nigga!"' she replied and we walked back into the hospital. Little was meeting us at the door.

"Bran and C got that nigga." was all he said, and I kissed Karter and turned back around out the door.

Moments later....

When I got to the warehouse, Little pulled to the back and I took my shirt off. It was mid-May so the weather was still hot.

"Who sent you?" I heard Chatlea say and then it went silent. My face turned up at the smell of flesh burning. As we got closer, I saw Charles with a torch in his hand lighting the nigga toes on fire.

"Bro, he gone start from the toes on up. Just tell him!" Brandon said smoking a blunt sitting right across from dude.

"No se que estas diciendo." *I don't know what you are saying*. He spoke in Spanish.

"Kill him." I said.

"No, no, no, no." He spoke in broken English.

"I thought you ain't know what we were saying." I laughed and walked toward him.

"Fuck you bastardo negro!" he said and spit towards my feet. Brandon grabbed his legs and pulled him making him fall backwards on his back. "Fuck!" He yelled out in pain. Charles took the blow torch and started on his feet again. When he passed out, Little went to the sink and grabbed a bucket of water. Throwing it on dude, he woke up gasping for air. Charles lit the blow torch up and dude act like he wanted to pass out again.

"Wakey wakey nigga!" Charles said and slapped him.

"Kill me!! I'M NOT TELLING YOU SHIT!" He said and

spat in Charles' face. Charles took the blow torch and started to torch his face. After his whole face was burned off, Charles emptied the clip into his face. I sighed and looked at Charles.

"I mean, I'mma just say this." He said and stopped talking when I looked at him.

"This got Ol chick written all over it. ol dude... Whoever the fuck they was... These they people!" He said interrupting me.

"Selena." Little said.

"Man, Why the fuck didn't I thin…" My phone vibrated, and it was a text from Karter.

"The results are in...."Congratulations." it read.

"FUCK!"

6

KARTER

I paced back and forth in Tiera's room waiting on Jamar to get back. Tiera was sleep, Eva had left to go back to our kids, and everyone else was gone. It was now eight in the morning, and I had texted Jamar over an hour ago. I didn't need to open it to know the results. That little girl was Jamar's kid. Shit, she looked just like our daughter Jamie, which would be Jamar's twin. Everything in me wanted to feel some type of way, but I really couldn't. She was before me but what the fuck!

I ripped the envelope open and read the results. She was indeed 99.9999998 his. I sighed and sat down. I knew the possibilities but it didn't hurt no less. Maybe because I feel like this was gone put us in a different position. He had another kid out here. Jamar accepted my kid with open arms, so what type of woman would I be to not accept his. I sighed and wiped the tears that had fallen. The door opened up and Markel walked from behind the curtain.

"I ain't know nobody was still here." he spoke. I liked Markel for Tiera. They fit perfectly and he calmed her down.

"I'm just gone step out right fast.... She should be waking up soon anyways." I told him and grabbed my purse. Soon as I walked into the waiting room, Ashley and Jamar's daughter was sitting there. Ashley was typing away on her phone, and their daughter was on her tablet. When Ashley saw me she stood up.

"Jamar's not here but I have the results." I told her and she nodded.

"I'm sorry. I'm not here to cause problems. I honestly don't even think about Jamar. I'm married, have been married for ten years, been with my husband since I was thirteen. My husband always thought our daughter wasn't his because of her features. He tested her without me knowing and finally told me after we had an argument. If you or Jamar don't want anything to do with me that's fine but I would love for y'all to have a relationship with her." she spoke and I nodded.

"We would love to have a relationship with her. It wouldn't be right to have his seed out here in the world when he's taking care of kids that's not his. I have two children also that's not biologically his. What's her name?" I asked.

"Ashtyn." Ashley called out to her daughter.

"Yes mommy." Ashtyn sweet voice spoke out. She stood next to her mother and my heart dropped. This little girl was Jamar's twin. From the curly hair, down to the nose.

"This Karter, your daddy wife." Ashley said and she smiled.

"Nice to meet you. I'm Ashtyn. I'm ten. I'll be eleven June first." Ashtyn spoke and I smiled.

"You so pretty." I complimented her and she smiled showing a toothless grin.

"Thank you. You are too. Do I have any sisters?" she

asked and I sat down next to her with Ashley on the other side.

"Yes, you have two sisters and two brothers." I told her and her eyes got big.

"Ew, I don't like boys. They are gross!" she said and I started to laugh.

"Yes every other boy is Gross except your brothers." I told her and she smiled.

"What's my brothers and sisters' name?" she asked me. I pulled out my phone showing her my screensaver.

"This is Kartier, but we call him KJ; he's eight. This Mariel, she's eight also. That's Jamie. She's five and that's Karson; he's ten months." I told her showing her pictures of my kids.

"I'm the oldest. Yess." Ashtyn said dragging out the s.

"I want to meet them and my daddy. Is he upset with me?" She asked and I sighed.

"Because when mommy said he was daddy, he cursed." she said and I smiled.

"No, your daddy isn't upset. He was just...." I couldn't find the words so I looked at Ashley.

"Your daddy just have a lot going on Ash. Remember when I said he didn't know about you? So he was just caught off guard." Ashley finished and I nodded.

"When you finally meet him y'all both are gonna love each other. He's a great guy and he loves all his children." I told her and she hugged me.

"Can I meet my brothers and sisters? Pleassse." she begged and I looked at Ashley.

"Of course." Ashley said and looked at me. Her phone started to ring and she stood up.

"It's work. I have to take this. Can you keep an eye on her?" She asked and I nodded.

"Can I tell you a secret Miss Karter?" Ashtyn asked me and I nodded.

"Of course. You can tell me whatever you want to." I replied.

"My mommy is very sick. My step father said mommy have to get better. Or mommy gone go to heaven like grandma." Ashtyn said. My heart dropped, and I sighed. Kids didn't know how much one little thing they said mattered. That's the same thing I had a problem with Mariel and Jamie and that's running they mouth.

"My other daddy left mommy, and now she's so sick she can't help me anymore."

she said and looked at me. Hearing all this made my heart go out for Ashley and Ashtyn. Kids was so smart; they listened and repeated every single thing. I know they don't know any better but god damn. I hugged Ashtyn because she was strong and smart, just like Jamar.

Jamar walked in with Charles, Little, Brandon, Marcel and Deno also behind him. His eyes was real low, so I knew he was high as hell. I prayed silently that he handled the problem. He looked from me to Ashtyn and I laughed. He looked so nervous and I felt bad.

"Bae, this is Ashtyn.... Ashtyn, this is your dad." I introduced them and he nodded. He sat down where we sat and Ashtyn stood up in front of him.

"I'm ten. Karter says I'm a big sister too." Ashtyn told Jamar and he smiled.

"Yes, you're are the oldest. You are very pretty." he told her and she giggled. I look like you silly." She giggled and hugged Jamar. He picked her up and looked around the room.

"Where's A.C.?" Jamar asked and I looked around too. I haven't even noticed that she hasn't come back yet. We both stood up when we saw nurses running down the hallway toward Teira's room.

"Stay here." Jamar told me as he followed Charles and Little.

"How about you put your headphones back on and play on your tablet." I told Ashtyn and she nodded and did what I told her. I stood up and told Brandon to watch her while I go look for Ashley. I went the opposite way and couldn't find her. When I went back to the emergency room, Jamar was standing there in a heated argument with a doctor.

"What's going on?" I asked them and they both looked at me.

"I'm the doctor that cared for Ashley Cain. She was admitted here maybe about three months ago. She was recently diagnosed with stage four lung cancer. She did all the treatments and her body is not quite strong enough to fight off the Cancer. I told this young man there's nothing we can do. I honestly believe that the treatments will kill her faster. With the treatments I give it two weeks... Without, I give it a month maybe two. I can't call it. I'm sorry sir. You are more than welcomed to see her." he said and walked away. *This what Ashtyn was talking about when she said her momma was sick.*

"I'm sorry Jamar." I told him reaching for his arm.

"I'm good." Jamar replied and followed the doctor to Ashley's room. I sighed and went back to the emergency room. I was getting Ashtyn and going home to my children. I guess I could introduce the kids to their new sibling.

7

ASHLEY

This is the first and the last time you'll ever see my chapter. Well maybe I'll get my own book, but until then I'll give you enough on my back story. Jamar and I never really had a relationship. When he first came into the prison, I was captured by his appearance off back. I mean, he was handsome as hell with beautiful eyes. Then getting to know him I fell in love. Yes, deeply in love to the point where my husband gave me an ultimatum: quit the prison or he was leaving me.

I kind of lied earlier. I didn't quit the prison until Jamar got released. Jamar knows we had been sleeping with each other up until he left. That's why he didn't deny Ash. I never tried to get in touch with Jamar when I found out I was pregnant because I knew he would want me to terminate my pregnancy. My husband and I knew Ashtyn wasn't his because he had a freak accident when he was twenty-one and couldn't have any children.

When I had Ashtyn and she came out with those eyes, I knew she was Jamar's, but he wasn't the only inmate I was fooling with. *That's another story for another day.* I was gone come out sooner but that's when everything went downhill, and I was diagnosed with stage three cancer. Did treatments for about three years or so then it went away. I wanted to be well and healthy for Jamar when I did come to him and finally tell him but the earth wouldn't let me be great, because a year later, I was diagnosed with stage three again.

I did chemo for a few months but it felt like it made it worse. So I declined and just wanted my body to fight the cancer itself. That's what I was doing at the hospital the day I met Karter. I was going to get a checkup because my body was shutting down on me. I couldn't eat. I was having uncontrollable bowel movements. The doctor told me the cancer had spread and it was untreatable, and I couldn't do anything about it. It took everything in me to be the bigger person because I knew I wanted Jamar to accept my daughter when it was my time to go. I also knew he was gone want a DNA test. I didn't want everybody to know my illness yet. My body was just shutting down faster than I thought.

Finally getting released out of the hospital, I walked to the Uber. The doctor didn't want me to leave, but I had to make sure my baby was okay and get her prepared for me leaving. It's been times were I talked to Ashtyn about what's going on with me. Let's be honest, no nine year old understands that her mother is dying, and it's nothing no one can do about it. I appreciate Jamar for taking her while I was in the hospital. I know I'mma be right back in a few days. I could feel it in my bones that I wouldn't be able to fight it off like the last times.

"Hello Miss Ashley. You have a lot of mail. Your mother just left yesterday." the doorman greeted and I nodded.

I took the elevator up to my suite and punched in my security code so it could open. The whole thirteenth floor was my apartment, and I loved it. I was leaving this to Ashtyn. Yes, I owned my penthouse. I owned everything I have. My husband is a wealthy celebrity lawyer, so when we divorced I got half of everything. Two cars, this suite, and a beach house in Florida. My husband and I are still great friends. He just wanted something that I wasn't willing to give him. Me. I can't even lie. Once I got a dose of Jamar it was like everything else didn't matter. I was making it my business to have him one last time or die trying.

SLIPPING into a spaghetti strap nightgown that came just below my butt, I oiled my legs down. I slipped my hair into a messy bun and applied lip gloss. Earlier when I got home I texted Jamar and told him we needed to talk now that I was out of the hospital, and he told me he would be here.

KNOCK. KNOCK. KNOCK.

Show time. I clapped my hands and skipped to the door. Jamar walked in looking fine as ever. He was wearing some blue Balmain jeans with a matching Balmain blue jean jacket and a white under shirt. He was rocking some custom made Retro Jordan's while he had on light jewelry.

"Thank you for coming. Come in." I opened my door wider and he walked in. Smelling good too. He was perfect.

"How's Ashtyn doing with the kids?" I asked sitting across from him while he was on the love seat.

"She's actually doing better than I thought. She's smart. You did a wonderful job with her." he told me and I smiled.

"I tried. I can't help but think I failed her in so many ways." I told him honestly. "I beat cancer once before I know I'm strong enough to do it again." he stood up and sat by me. He pulled my hands into his.

"Don't worry about that shawty. We gone make sure you

spend all the time with her and we gone make sure she know how much you love her." he said and I nodded. "I wished you would have told me about her sooner so I could've been a part of y'all life sooner." Jamar said and I felt like shit now.

"I tried finding you. It was so hard with me being sick and going through a divorce. I had so much going on." I responded.

"I feel like shit cause you my baby moms and I don't know shit about you. Tell me about you though." He awkwardly laughed. We sat and talked and after about an hour of just filling him in on what was going on in my life he decided to order some pizza. After the pizza came, we chilled, ate, and talked more. It was going on two o'clock in the morning when he finally decided he wanted to leave. I talked him into staying a night, and he could sleep on the couch. He agreed and we went to sleep. Well, I couldn't go to sleep so I got naked and went to the front room. Jamar was knocked out laying on his back with his hand in his pants. I snuggled up against him and he wrapped his arms around me. This all I ever wanted to be. I drifted to sleep peacefully.

8

KRIS

When I pulled up to my house that I now shared with Bran and our three daughters I knew something was wrong. Ever since I got shot a few years back, I have been having these feelings every single time something was going on. My gut never was wrong. I dialed Eva number and she answered after the first ring.

"How's the kids?" I asked soon as she said hello.

"They're sleep girl. What's going on?" She asked me.

"Nothing I'm just making sure they okay. I'll call you in."

Before I could even finish my sentence gunshots rang out. Even though my whole truck was bulletproof, it still didn't stop me from getting on the floor shielding myself. It seem like the shots just kept coming because only time it stopped is when I heard the sirens. My door yanked open and I saw Brandon's face. The tears started to flow at that point.

"Shorty it's okay." He grabbed and hugged me.

"Brandon.... Oh my god." I cried out and hugged him tightly.

"You okay ma. I got you shorty." He kept repeating as he took me out of my car.

....

"Girl shit, you scared the fuck out of me!" Eva said once we walked into her house. The kids were all sleep and Eva was in the kitchen making coffee. Jamar walked in with Little and Charles.

"You okay sis?" Jamar asked hugging me. I nodded and sighed.

"I'm good. Did y'all pull the tapes?" I asked.

"We got Mace on it right now." Jamar told me and I nodded. "We gotta send out shipments in the morning. So in the morning y'all gone pack the kids up. Tiera come home tomorrow. Everybody has security on them at all times!" Jamar told me.

"This is too much. We got muthafuckas trying to kill us every time we step foot out of the house. I'm scared to send my kids to fucking school on Monday!" I said and looked at Brandon then Jamar. "Fix this shit. FAST!" I yelled at Brandon and walked away.

When I got upstairs to the room my kids were sleeping. I climbed into bed behind Brylynn and snuggled up against my daughter. Braylon and Britton was on the other bed sprawled out. My daughters was my everything. Bray and Bry just turned eight and was grown as hell. Britt on the other hand is a momma's girl and just turned six.

Braylon looked just like me and Bry looked just like Brandon. Brit looked like both of us. With all this going on I still haven't had the time to tell Brandon I was six weeks pregnant. I wasn't showing at all and still had time to think about if I was keeping it or not. Every marriage have they problems but as soon as we got married our problems came. When he divorced his wife I thought everything was going to be okay with us. That was the least of my problems, from the cheating to the drug usage to the abuse. I didn't think we would go through all this so early in our marriage. That's exactly what we get though. Everybody around us was getting married and happy so we hopped on the bandwagon and didn't know who the hell we were marrying.

Now we're both unhappy. Not willing to call it quits because of the time and children we invested. I knew it was over when we both had to be intoxicated with something to be around each other. Liquor was my choice. Cocaine was his. I didn't judge. If he liked it, I loved it. As long as he didn't let the shit he did come to our doorstep I was fine.

"Mommy, you okay?" Britt asked turning my way wiping my eyes.

"Yes mommy is really tired. Go to sleep." I told her and kissed her forehead. She rolled back over and we both drifted back to sleep.

I DIDN'T WAKE up until about twelve o'clock in the afternoon the next day. When I came to, I heard yelling downstairs. The kids were already up so I gathered myself and went to see what the hype was.

"So you had a whole fucking kid out here and never knew!" Eva yelled.

"Yes ma. She came to the hospital the other day. Man it's more to it. The girl is sick and dying soon." Jamar said and Eva sighed.

"Everything cool? " I asked making my presence noticed.

"Oh god. You're still here?" Eva said and looked from me to the entrance of the kitchen.

"Yes. Where's the kids?" I asked and stood against the door way.

"I had Marcel and Deno take them to Karter. So we could get going to the house." Jamar said.

"Come on; go get dressed and I'll take you over there." Eva said and tried to usher me upstairs. She followed me but I stopped mid-stride when I heard Brandon laugh and then a woman laugh. I sighed and walked right back downstairs. Everybody knew about the random woman cheated on me with. If it was a bitch he was fucking in this house, it was definitely gone be some shit! When I walked into the living room, a chick was sitting in his lap and he was whispering in her ear.

"Excuse me!" I yelled. When he noticed it was my voice he pushed her onto the floor off his lap. "Who the fuck is this Brandon?" I asked and he just stood up looking stupid.

"Uhm.... Uhm." He stuttered. " I thought you left this morning with the kids." his stupid ass finally said. I charged at him swinging wildly. Brandon tried to grab my arms but my hands were too fast. I kept swinging until I felt Jamar grab me from behind picking me up.

"I'mma fuck both y'all up!" I yelled still swinging and fighting the air at this point. Jamar was not letting me go with his cocky ass! "Get the fuck off me!" I yelled. Jamar dropped me on my ass and I stood up.

"This how the fuck y'all do me? Fuck y'all!" I shouted. I went by knocking all the vases down on my way out the door. "Fuck Brandon! Fuck this fucked up ass family. I hope all they asses get blown to fucking pieces." I yelled getting into my truck driving the fuck away from there!

9

MACE

"You cool sis? Whenever you need me, I don't care what time it is, call me!" I voiced.

"I know. I was scared as hell! I thought I was dead this time." Kris said and looked at me.

"Don't say that shit. I'm on it so whoever did that shit gone pay." I told her.

This was the second time my little sister got shot at, and I wasn't having it. My sisters was going thru some shit behind the niggas they loved. I respected them for sticking with they niggas but damn! That's why nobody knew my personal life. Only people who knew about anything I got going on was Mason, and that's because my bro was my other half. I be damned if any nigga in the streets used my family to get back at me.

"Look, I got you and, as long as I'm here, that's all that matters. I ain't going nowhere." I told Kris and she smiled.

"Thanks bro." She hugged me, and I went downstairs to see what my Madukes was doing. Being in and out of state, graduated college and working for BFG, I was always on the go! My home was Nap-town, but I ain't live there for no longer than three month. Then I was back out into the world.

"I'm glad you came. Mason on his way and should be here soon." My mom spoke.

"I know ma. We gone come back home more. Shit, I can't believe these niggas back in that stupid shit again." I voiced, and she shook her head.

"I pray these niggas don't get my babies ran up. I know y'all and Jamar gone protect them but damn. I'm still thinking about the time I got the call that Kri was shot!" she said and sat down at the kitchen table.

"Just bear with me. I'mma figure out who was behind this." I told her and she smiled.

"How has work been?" my mother asked and I smiled. My mother didn't know I worked for Jamar and the Black Guerrilla Family. She just thought I went to school to play ball and that I lived in another state with some chick. None of that was true. I worked out of state, usually in Florida, and I was they Technology Guy.

Ring, ring, ring.

"Ma, I gotta take this call but I'mma be outside." I told her and walked away.

"Hello." I answered.

"Hey honey. I just picked up Montana from school. How is the family?" My wife Bria spoke, and I smiled.

"They good. My sisters just got caught up in the mix of they husbands' shit." I told her and leaned up against my car.

"I hope she's okay. How's your mother?" Bria asked, and I pressed the FaceTime button on my phone so I could see my wife and kids. My wife was beautiful as hell. Dark skinned standing about 5'6, Bria was kind of on the heavy side. Nonetheless, she was gorgeous. She carried her weight perfectly also. Her hair was the natural curly that most chicks paid for. It fell to the middle of her back. She had deep dimples on each cheek, and that was what drew me into her. Most of the times, she was classy as hell, but I saw the ratchetness under all that.

"Babe, are you gonna be home for dinner? I was thinking steak, scallop potatoes, and pasta salad. What do you think?" She asked. "Babe?" she called out to me and I laughed.

"Sorry bae, I'm daydreaming. What did you say?" I wondered and she rolled her eyes.

"I was asking how's your mother?" she sighed.

"She's fine. Worried about her children but she's fine. How was Tana's day?" I asked and she smirked.

"Just forget what I say." she mumbled and passed the phone back to Montana my seven-year-old son.

"Hey dad. Where are you?" he asked soon as he saw my face.

"I'm visiting your grandma. Your auntie hasn't been feeling well so I had to come check on her." I told Montana, and he frowned and sighed.

"When am I going to see my aunty dad? I wanna see her and grandma." he said and I sighed.

"Very soon. How was school?" I asked and he smiled.

"It was fun. Can you come get me?" Montana asked and looked at Bria.

"Yes, I'll come get you, and we'll go to the park and get ice cream." I told him and he started to smile.

"Yes dad. Okay, come on now." He told me and handed his momma back the phone.

"My dad called and said he wanted us to come over tomorrow night; he needs to speak to us." she spoke and I sighed.

"Is it business or personal?" I asked and she laughed. "When is it ever not business with that man?" She asked and I nodded.

"Okay... that's cool." I smiled, and she glanced at the screen then back at the road.

"You so fine." she told me, and I smirked.

"Girl, don't tell me that." I blushed.

"Boy, you blushing?" she laughed, and my baby Brielle started to cry.

"What's wrong with my baby?" I asked and she sighed.

"She's a spoiled brat." Bria replied.

"Well, let me get off here cause we just pulled up to the spot." Bria said and I nodded.

"Alright, I love y'all. I should be home in about an hour." I told her, and we disconnected the call. I sat on my porch and contemplated on telling my family about my wife. I decided not to and just wait it out. I know shit was getting heavy with the family, and I wasn't putting my wife and seeds into the mix of this shit! We already had a lot of shit on our plates, and BGF issues wasn't getting ready to be added either.

10

MASON

"Look, I told you what it was when we first started fucking. Don't do too much shorty!" I hissed stepping into my pants and grabbing my shirt.

"I mean, yeah, you said you not ready for a relationship. That was well over a year ago Mason. Shit, you kept me around. I thought we were building something." Lashawn said.

"You couldn't have thought that." I yelled not wanting to hear anything else. "Brah listen. You cool and all, but I don't want to be with you. I understand if you caught feelings or whatever, but I'm good on a relationship. It's not you... it's me." I said and grabbed my pistol and phone walking out. I jumped into my new Expedition truck and banged out the parking lot, firing a blunt soon as I got on the highway.

I was happy today because I was finally leaving Michigan and going back home. I decided to drive because I wanted to clear my head, and it was only about four hours there if I'm driving.

Ring. Ring. Ring.

"What it do?" I answered.

"You on the road yet?" Mace asked once I answered the phone.

"Yeah bro. I'm still in the city though. Wassup?" I asked and he sighed.

"Shit, just chilling. We got some shit we need to handle like ASAP." He vented.

"Alright, that's coo. How's the wifey?" I asked and he laughed.

I was the only one that knew my brother was married with kids. He wanted to keep it a secret for her sake and his. Mace and I always been close. He knew my secrets and I knew his. We were best friends on top of brothers.

"She good. I might need you to keep the kids tonight while I take B out." Mace said and I laughed. "As long as you keep yo little chicken heads away." he threw in making me laugh.

"I got you big bro, and besides, I'm leaving everybody in Michigan." I told him and he smacked his lips.

"Whatever you say. So how long you got?" he asked and I looked at the GPS screen.

"Three hours and twenty-seven minutes."

"Alright bet," Mason responded.

"You gone tell them?" He asked and I laughed.

"Yeah, when I feel the time is right." I told him and he agreed. We discussed some more things about the business and what we decided to do about the BGF, then disconnected the call. I dialed Kris number but she ain't answer. Pulling off the highway, I pulled to the gas station, got some snacks and filled my tank up. I was never stepping foot in Michigan again. *I hate it here!*

11

JANIA

"If he ask, I'm not here. Say I dropped the kids off and kept going." I sighed sipping my wine.

"Girl, you can't hide out here forever!" Karter said as she chopped up fruit for the kids. We both heard a loud crash and dashed to the living room where the kids were supposed to be watching T.V. When we came into view, the 60-inch that they kept hanging on the wall was now on the floor.

"How the fu...." Karter started to say but the kids yelling telling who made the TV fall over talked her.

"Shut the fuck up!" Karter yelled.

"Get the fuck over here!" I yelled to TJ. He instantly started to cry, which gave me the answer on who broke the T.V.

"No Tete. She kept pushing him so he grabbed the cord on accident to stop from falling." Mariel said Pointing at Ty'Aira.

"Come here." I told her and she started crying also. I grabbed the belt off the back of the couch and tore both they asses up. "Now go lay the fuck down!" I yelled, and they both walked away crying looking like they ugly ass daddy.

"I should beat they ass next!" Karter said, and I laughed because everybody knows Karter is the parent that don't whoop her kids.

"I'mma have they daddy beat they ass too. They fucking know better. They don't dare do that shit at my house!" I told her straight up. We went back to the kitchen where Karter was cooking. She separated the fruit on different plates and called the kids to the kitchen table so they could eat they lunch.

"After y'all done eating go find y'all a fucking spot on the floor and go to sleep!" Karter said and nobody said nothing.

"Mama Karter…. I'm allergic to peanut butter." Ashtyn called out, and Karter looked at her.

"Shit, sorry daughter. I forgot." Karter said grabbing the plate tossing it in the trash. She went back over to the counter to fix Ashtyn something else to eat. After feeding the kids, which was about twelve kids, they all laid down on the floor and went to sleep like Karter said. None of the kids played with Karter because they were all scared of Jamar.

"How can you do it?" I asked as I helped her clean up the mess the kids did.

"What? Watch all these kids? Well, with my four and then Ashtyn, it's not hard cause usually she helps me with Karson. KJ be in his own world, and Mariel and Jamie is combined at the hip so they be in they own world too. With everything going on with Ashley, Ash is connected to my hip." she said and I looked at her.

"Yeah, I mean how can you be okay with raising her. Like, I don't know. I just feel so disgusted and hurt." I started to say but Karter shook her head.

"Sorry sis, you can't compare you and Little situation to

ours. Just like Ty'aira was way before you, Ash was before me, so I have no choice but to accept her! It's only right. Jamar adopted KJ and everything. He also loves the shit out of Mariel, and she's neither of ours! I love Ash like she's my own because she's from the man I love. Little fucked up. Do you think marriages last by throwing it away every single time either of us mess up? You married this man knowing he WAS deeply in love with his baby mama. You married this man knowing he cheated on his baby mama with someone, and that's why they're not together now. So what, you're gonna leave him and mess with him on the low?" She asked me, and I rolled my eyes.

"Girl, first of all, fuck you okay." I said and we laughed.

"These nasty ass kids.." Karter said picking up some candy that was stuck to her floor.

"I mean, bitch, it is what, one, two, three........ Eleven kids here." I said and she sat down.

"So how is Jamar with this whole new kid thing?" I questioned.

"I mean, he hasn't really had the time to even spend with her. When he comes home, she's either on her way to sleep or already in bed. When he wakes up, she isn't even up yet. I just want him to spend time with her. She's already losing her mother. She needs him the most now." She replied back to me.

"Speaking of that. How's that going?" I asked.

Every single day, it was different drama going on within everyone. We never really come together like that anymore, cause every time we all together some shit pop off. So now the guys stick the kids with somebody during the day and today was Karter and my day. It's been two weeks since Tiera got shot and as much as I hate her ass right now I'm glad she isn't dead. Little and myself haven't said not one word to each other. I was missing him like crazy, but I'm glad it's the way it is.

"Enough about my problems. How are you handling everything? You been feeling okay?" Karter asked me and I sighed.

"I didn't go through with it." I told her.

"Wow, so you still is right now?" she asked me to look at my stomach.

"Yes bitch. I couldn't do it. As much as he hurt me and I hate him, I'm not killing my baby! Why should I have to kill my kid and she's having one." I told her feeling myself getting emotional.

"It's not about her. Are you ready for another kid?" Karter asked me and I sighed.

"I'm not. Ty is barely one. What the hell I'mma do with another fucking kid? If I would of went on with it, I would be doing it out of hurt and spite. I can't do it right now." I told her. "I was thinking about talking to Little first then going on from there." I said and Karter nodded.

Ring. Ring. Ring.

Her phone started to ring, and she got up to go grab it. While she checked her phone, I went upstairs to check on Ty and Karson. They both were still sleep so I went back downstairs. I had a lot to think about and this little baby growing inside of me was clouding my judgement.

Few hours later....

"Alright. Just call me in the morning." Karter told Kris as she strapped her kids in the car. We waved and shut the door as she drives off.

"I missed you too." Little said to T-Two making me roll my eyes. His voice was so annoying and disturbing.

"Can you please come home now." Tyree Jr said, and I sighed. I gathered Ty's stuff and sat by the door. "Alright friend. Y'all be careful and call me when y'all get home." Karter said and we hugged.

"Bye Tete mans." she said kissing Ty and then doing the same to TJ and Ty'aira.

"Bye bro." I told Jamar and left out with Little carrying TJ in his arms after I strapped Ty in. I got in the front seat. He clicked TJ in and came to my side. I let my window down and he leaned in.

"My sons want me to come over tonight. So I'mma stop by if that's okay with you?" He asked. I rolled my eyes and looked at Little.

"That's fine with me." I told him and he smiled. "We have to talk about something anyways." I added and he nodded.

"Alright, I'll see y'all later then." he said and tried to kiss my lips, but I moved my face and rolled my window up. I drove home contemplating on giving in to Little or not. I decided not to and just wait. If he wanted me back then he would have to work for it. He definitely wasn't getting off that easy, but I definitely wasn't letting go of my marriage. Maybe marriage counseling would be in the works.

12

BRANDON

"You don't give a fuck about me! You don't give a fuck about us." Kris yelled.

"Man, shut the fuck up before you wake my kids up!" I hissed getting into her face.

"Yo kids? Nigga, you ain't shit to them. All yo ass do is run the streets, fuck different bitches and smoke up all yo shit! You ain't shit nigga!" She yelled pushing me.

My reflex made me slap the shit out of her, and she came back with a punch. We went blow for blow for a second until I knocked her ass down and dazed her. Kris' mouth was bleeding and I had scratches on my face and neck.

"Fuck you Brandon!" she yelled getting up walking away.

I pulled the baggie out my pocket and opened it. I slipped my pinky into the substance and put it to my nose inhaling it all off my pinky. After the high took over me, I went to the kitchen where I knew Kris would be. She was pouring herself a drink and putting ice on her eye.

"That's all you give a fuck about is the bottle huh?" I asked her.

"Nah nigga. I give a fuck about my kids, my motherfucking sister and brothers bitch! Can I say the same about you?" she yelled.

"All you care about is that white shit around your nose! Do you even give a fuck that a muthafucka came to OUR fucking house? Where OUR kids lay at and shot at me. Did you even pull the cameras to even see?" she yelled getting upset, which instantly made me feel like shit. With all this other shit going on she was right. I never sent Mace over here to check the cameras to see who the fuck shot at her.

"Look, I tried holding on. We got married too fast trying to keep up with my sister and Jamar and it's made me, us very unhappy! You fuck with other women so many times I lost count. I'm done Brandon. I'm so done. I been done... I have been trying to save face but this not working." she said and walked away. I shrugged my shoulder, dipped my pinky finger into my sack, and put it to my nose. I was easing my mind tonight and dealing with the world tomorrow.

"Daddy, daddy?" Britt yelled waking me up. I groaned when I rolled over and noticed it was just now hitting seven-thirty. I just went to sleep at four.

"We hungry daddy." Bray said tapping me.

"Wake mommy up and tell her." I yawned rolling back around closing my eyes.

"Mommy gone. Mommy car not here either." Brit said and tapped me again. "We hungry." Britton whined and I rolled out of bed.

"Go to the kitchen and I'll be there." I told them and they ran out the room. Blowing out my breath, I went to the bathroom to handle my hygiene. Bags was forming under my eyes, and I looked like I was up partying last night. I shook my head and finished handling my hygiene. I went downstairs to the kitchen. The two oldest was sitting at the table.

"Where baby girl?" I asked referring to Brylynn.

"She's with mommy." Britton said.

"Cereal it is." I told my girls.

"No Daddy, Mommy only let us have cereal on Saturdays." Brit told me ,and I looked at her.

"How you know what today is?" I asked her.

"Daddy, I'm not a baby. And look, every day mommy teach us." Brit said pointing to the poster on the wall. "Okay, how about we have cereal today, and it's our little secret." I said and fixed them both some cereal. I sat down next to them while they ate. I didn't have an appetite. So I tried calling Kris number but it went to voicemail.

"When y'all done go get dressed." I told them and went upstairs to get in the shower. After showering, I slipped on some sweatpants and slides with a white shirt. I went to the kids' room and they were fully dressed in something simple, so we left. When I got into the car, I dialed Mace up.

"Hello?" He answered on the fourth ring.

"Nigga, I need a huge favor." I said.

"Nigga, it's eight in the morning and you calling about a favor." he asked. The phone went silent and he hung up. I laughed and pulled up to my Aunty Eva crib.

Ring. Ring. Ring.

"Bitch ass nigga did you just hang up on me?" I asked once Mace called back.

"Go in the house, sit down, and watch T.V." I told the girls, and they hopped out my truck and ran to the door.

"I need you to pull the cameras at my crib ASAP!" I told him and he groaned.

"Fuck! How's sis??" He asked and I sighed.

"I don't know where her ass at. We got into it and she left. We getting a divorce bro." I told him straight up.

"Not my problem. Not my problem. Not my problem." he kept saying and hung up. I shook my head and got out the car. When I entered Aunty Eva house, she was in the kitchen cooking breakfast.

"Hey aunty." she mugged me and kept moving around the kitchen.

"Boy, don't hey me. I don't know what you got going on in that big ass head of yours. You know what, I don't know what the hell none of you niggas got going on around this bitch. Yo ass up here beating the girl, cheating on the girl, and who the fuck knows what else. Jamar ditzy ass bringing home grown ass kids. Tiera dumb ass getting pregnant AGAIN by a married ass man... Charles...... Shit, Charles the only normal muthafucka. Y'all gone send me to an early grave. I swear to God if it's not these kids tearing up my fucking house, it's y'all and y'all bullshit. I'm sick of y'all." she yelled.

"Y'all muthafuckas got so much fucking shit going on y'all can't even take care of y'all kids properly and see who the fuck is trying to kill y'all!" she yelled slamming the dish down. "Take yo kids and get the fuck out." she told me.

"But......but aunty." I stuttered. She gave me a look and pointed to the door. I shook my head and called out to my kids. I guess everybody was sick and fed up with my shit.

13

KARTER

With everything going on with people trying to kill us and everybody at each other's throat, I just decided to have all the family get together.

KNOCK. KNOCK. KNOCK.

I turned the stove on low and headed to the door. Jamar was downstairs in the basement probably smoking or whatever. I looked out the peephole and saw Mason. Today was the first time I laid eyes on him since he left home a few years ago. Pulling the door opens I jumped in his arms.

"Dang Kar, You not a baby no-more." he laughed hugging me.

"I missed you so much.... Look at you Mason." I smiled. My brother was all grown up. Tall as ever and cocky as hell with facial hair. "Oh my god Mason." I laughed hugging my brother again.

"Girl, don't be acting like you don't see nobody!" Kris said pushing through us. Kris walked in, followed by Brit, Bray and Brylynn. My mother Janet and little brother Chubby came right after them.

"Welcome you guys. Welcome." I opened the door wider for them to come in.

"Aw, there go Mace sis." Mason said looking out the door as an all black-on-black Range Rover pulled up. Mace stepped out and walked to the passenger side.

"Who he got with him?" I asked and Mason smiled big.

"Oh shit." He whispered, and I rolled my eyes.

"Boy who that?" My brother Chubby asked and I shrugged.

"Let me go meet my nieces and nephews." He switched off. I mean, switched for real. I had to take a double take because the nigga was walking like a straight female.

"Lord Jesus." I mumbled. Looking back out the door, I was caught off guard when Mason had a baby in one arm on the other a pretty ass female smiling.

"I know this nigga didn't pop out with a family." Kris said from behind us.

"Hey wassup y'all? This is Bria, my wife. This is Montana and Brielle." He said all in one breath and my momma clapped.

"About time. Shit I was tired of acting like I didn't know." Janet said, and I looked at her then Mace.

"You knew?" we both asked and they walked in.

"It's finally nice to meet you. I have heard so much about you." Bria spoke and we hugged.

"It's nice to meet you also." I spoke, surprised that my brother was actually married with children.

"You so cute. How old are you?" I wondered. He was the spitting image of Mace, and he was just so handsome.

"I'm six." he said with a toothless grin.

"You are so cute." I cooed kissing his cheeks... It's kids upstairs you can go play with." I told Montana, and he looked at Mace for approval and ran off.

"Well dang bro. You could've told me!" I said as we all walked back to the kitchen where I poured everyone something to drink and finished cooking. Jamar walked in with Karson in his hands.

"Hey, what's up everybody?" he spoke and kissed me on my cheek. My husband was so handsome and even though we haven't been seeing eye to eye I prayed daily that God see us through this hard time.

"Aw what's up Sis?" he spoke and all our attention went to Bria and him.

"How y'all know each other?" Mace asked and Bria laughed.

"Jamar? Man, what is up?" she asked and they hugged.

"Wow babe, I didn't know this who you were talking about." She told Mace, and he nodded.

"I been trying to reach out to pops; he ain't been fucking with me." Jamar said and Bria sat down.

"I actually been needing to talk to you about that. Daddy stepped down. I run his organization now.... Mace and myself." she said and everybody looked at Mace.

"That's what's up bro. I'm proud of y'all man! Y'all got y'all hands full with them crazy ass Russians!" Jamar said and dapped Mace up. *Russians? I thought they had a thing against Black people.*

"Oh nigga I know. They weren't pleased when they found out I was stepping in and helping B." He said and Jamar sat across from them.

"So what, y'all a couple? Little sis got a baby?" Jamar said and handed Karson to Mason who just walked into the kitchen.

"What's up lil bro. How you been?" he asked Mason and Mason shrugged.

"Can't complain. So everybody got acquainted?" he asked and I nodded.

KNOCK. KNOCK. KNOCK

"I got it." I spoke to Jamar as he tried to get up. Looking out the windows, I saw it was the rest of the family. "Hey guys. Hey y'all." Eva spoke and hugged everyone.

"The kids upstairs." I told them as they raced to the stairs and walked back to the kitchen to finish cooking.

Once Jamar side got here, it was awkward as hell. Tiera and Jania was beefy as hell and wanted all smoke with each other. Brandon and Kris was sitting far away from each other. If looks could kill Brandon a be a dead motherfucka. Charles was in deep thought. Not really talking which was odd, too, because everybody know Charles was the life of the party. Little was irritated as hell because Tiera kept making baby jokes. I know if somebody doesn't speak up soon it was gonna be World War Three. I stood up.

"Excuse me. Okay, I called everyone here, because I know we all have problems and it's a lot of stuff going on. I just wanted the family to get back to how we used to be, no drama, no fighting each other. I wanted to start first and say thank you Jamar. Ever since you came into my life you have loved me like no other and accepted me with all my bullshit. You have carried this family and you are the glue that holds us all together. I love you." I said and sat down.

"I love you too." he said and kissed my lips.

Electric shot thru my body. That was the first affection he showed me in a long time, and I was grateful for that. Nobody else said anything. Everybody just started back eating and shit; the tension was still in the air. Eva stood up and sighed.

"I have something to say. I mean, since nobody else

wants to address the elephant in the room. Then guess I have to." Eva said and looked at Jamar.

"Y'all niggas!" Eva pointed at each and every one of the men in attendance. Marcel and Deno even brought their girls Tegan and Ana with them.

"You niggas sitting here like y'all don't feel these women energy. Y'all fucking married them! Some of y'all running round here like y'all not. I wish my husband was here right now. God bless his soul. I'm sick of this, and I'm sick of taking care of y'all kids too! You niggas leaving ya women and kids to tip and run the streets all day long. Don't come home days at a time. Dummies bringing babies home. GETTING PREGNANT BY OTHER MARRIED MEN! Listen, you know why y'all can't get to the bottom of who want y'all dead? Karma. Because y'all out here moving dirty." Eva said and Tiera stood up.

"Sit yo ass down. NOW!" Eva yelled and Tiera sat right back down. "I don't know what's gotten into y'all. But y'all better fix it. Before one of us not here to fix it." she said and sat down.

"Well damn." Charles said and laughed. I shook my head and everybody finished eating.

Later that night......

"Dad can you call my mommy?" Ashtyn asked Jamar. He looked at me, and I turned the other way. "How about I take you to go see her tomorrow?" He asked and she smiled.

"Can my brothers and sisters come too?" She asked.

"Yes of course." he told her and she hugged him.

"Go get ready for bed." Jamar told her, then she hugged me next and ran off.

"That little girl is smart as hell Jamar. She's really advanced." I told him and he nodded.

"I know. I don't know what I'mma do with her." he said. I

went downstairs to go check on Kris; she was laying down in the bed in our guest room.

"Hey sis, you okay?" I knocked.

"I'm good. What's up?" she asked sitting up.

"Just checking on you. I saw how you were at the dinner and you and Bran didn't say anything to each other. What's going on?" I asked her and she sighed.

"Brandon and I are divorcing. I mean, we both are unhappy. It's going to take a lot for us to get back to being happy with each other." she sadly said. Kris wiped her tears that fell and I hugged her. "It's just so much, and I don't even want to talk about it. I go look at this apartment tomorrow. So we will be out y'all hair soon. Plus, I'm still scared as hell from getting shot at and right now I just want to remove me and my kids from the situation." she told me and I nodded.

"I agree. Well, I'm not in a rush. I like having y'all here. Just like old times." I said and we both lightly laughed.

"Well goodnight." I told her and exited the room. After checking on KJ, he was knocked out. So I walked through the connected bathroom to Jamie and Mariel's room, and they both were knocked out also. I stopped by Ashtyn's room, and she slept with Karson snuggled up against her. I smiled. Ever since Ashtyn came to live with us full time, she act like Karson was her son. He slept with her every night. Some nights she brought his fussy butt to me, though, which I didn't mind. I went to my room, and Jamar was knocked out. I went to shower for about twenty-five minutes. I dried off and oiled and hygiene my body down. Entering our bedroom, I was caught off guard by Jamar slipping on some black sweatpants along with a matching all-black hoodie. I sighed and sat down on the bed.

"Leaving?" I asked pretty much already knowing the answer.

"Yeah.... Mace got addresses on the video when Kris got shot at. He said it's some Jamaican cats." he said and looked at me as he finished getting dressed. I nodded and laid down. Jamar came to me and kissed my lips.

"I love you dearly Jamar." I told him and he smirked.

"I love you too shorty." he kissed my lips again, this time with a little more tongue. I said a prayer for my man and family before I drifted to sleep.

I felt my bed dip down in the middle of the night and felt taps.

"Mommy Karter, can we sleep with you please?" Ashtyn whined as she sat Karson on my chest.

"Yes, of course." I yawned. I moved over a little and put Ashtyn on one side and Karson on the other.

"I had a scary dream. I miss my mommy." Ashtyn cried as I pat her back.

"It's okay. We gone go visit mommy. So you can see her and tell her how you been." I told her and she nodded.

"Okay." she whispered and we both drifted to sleep. My alarm went off at exactly eight o'clock. Karson was at the other end knocked out, and Ashtyn was crawled up on Jamar's chest knocked out. I said a quick prayer thanking God that he brought Jamar back home to us. I slid out of bed unannounced and handled my hygiene first. I went downstairs to check on Kris and the girls but they were gone. After starting my breakfast for my family, I went to start a load of laundry.

Ring, ring, ring!

I hesitated to answer the private call so I let it ring and go to voicemail. I turned my food on low and went to the house phone to call Mace. He answered on the first ring.

"Hello?" he answered groggily.

"Mace, track my phone call. They gone be calling in the

next two minutes. They just called. I didn't answer but usually when I don't answer they call back in five minutes." I whispered all in one breath.

"Got you sis." he said and hung up. Standing up, my phone rung. Private call.

"Who is this?" I asked.

"Don't worry about it bitch! You took something from me, so it's only right I do the same. I'm gonna make your life a living hell until y'all catch me. Which will be never." the caller said and laughed.

"Who is this?" I asked again.

"Your worst nightmare." they taunted and hung up.

"Fuck!" I yelled and threw my phone down.

Ring, Ring, Ring.

"Who the..."

"It's me, man." Mace said on the other end.

"Sorry bro." I said and sighed.

"Look I don't know who it was. Y'all have to be talking for at least a minute." He responded.

"Fuck." I hissed as I finished cooking.

"Don't worry. Jamar got this sis. You just worry about them kids." Mace said and I agreed. My brother and I chopped it up for a while until my kids started to come down one by one. After I finished cooking, I disconnected the call with Mace and fixed my kids some food. Jamar and Karson came down followed by Ash. After fixing everyone's plate, we all sat down at the table eating. This was the first time in a while eating breakfast with Jamar so I made pancakes, turkey bacon, white rice, and turkey sausage with fresh fruit. It was silent for the most part. Everyone was too busy eating.

"So daddy, are you taking us to see my mom today?" Ashtyn asked after she took a bite.

"Actually, I have a lot of stuff to do today. I was hoping I could take you some other time." Jamar said looking at me then at Ashtyn. I set my fork down and folded my arms across my chest.

"Oh okay." Ashtyn replied back clearly sad about him not taking her. Ashtyn picked her fork up but quickly put it back down and excused herself. After all the other kids finished eating, I cleaned the table and gathered Karson so I could bathe him. Jamar followed me.

"So you not talking to me or something?" he asked and I rolled my eyes.

"Everything just so important.... you haven't even spent fucking time with yo kids Jamar. That little girl barely even know you! Today was the first time in a whole month that she ate breakfast with you!" I yelled.

"I'm trying to make shit better for US! THAT'S WHY I AIN'T HERE! I got muthafuckas gunning for us that I don't even know who the hell they are! A muthafucka can run up in this bitch right now." he yelled getting into my face.

"Okay and when they do, yo ass won't be here! Cause you never here!" I yelled back getting pissed off at this point.

"I'm here now ain't I?" he asked.

"For how long? An hour? Can't even take YOUR fucking daughter to see her mother! Fuck you Jamar! Go run the streets and do what you do! Get Karson out the bath too!" I yelled walking past him to the girls' room. After I gathered the girls' clothes, I went to Kartier room and did the same.

Once I got out the shower, I slipped on my underclothes and slipped on some white Capris, with a white matching Bebe tank top with the white diamonds. On my feet was some white and silver Chanel slides. I slipped my hair into a messy bun and added lip gloss after gathering my son's diaper bag and gathering my purse. I went to the girls' room.

Jamie, Mariel, and Ashtyn was dressed in a pink, green, light blue and white Ralph Lauren dresses with some matching Ralph Lauren sandals. Their hair was freshly braided courtesy of Kris... Kartier and Karson had on red and white Ralph Lauren shirts with some black Levi jeans. On they feet was some white, red, and a dash of black Jordan Retro fourteens.

I gathered all my kids and we headed to the door. My first stop was Charles' shop to get this wig done and then I was taking Ash to see her mother. Then we were going to the park or somewhere. When we got outside, I gathered all my kids into my Jeep. Jamar came walking out of the house fully dressed.

"So you wasn't gonna say bye?" he asked and I laughed.

"Bye Jamar. Say bye to y'all daddy." I told my kids as I shut my door. He peeked his head into my window and they all waved and said bye.

"Marcel will be following you today. You good?" he asked and I rolled my eyes.

"Bye Jamar." I shouted backing up out the garage and driving away. He was definitely on my shit list for today.

....

"Girl yes, married boo. Ten fucking plus years! We eight years in so that nigga must been cheating their whole marriage!" Charles yelled and looked at me through the mirror. I knew he was hurt but tried to act hard. Charles was the protective one out of everybody! He didn't play about us and definitely could murk a nigga in a minute.

"Damn C. I know that shit got you sick!" Tiera replied and I rolled my eyes. Tiera was cool but Jania was my bitch period. I ain't have shit to do with what they all had going on but I wasn't gone be friendly either. I definitely wasn't feeling her playing my bitch like that.

"Ten years? He's weak for that. So did you ask about that?" I asked.

"Nope. I'mma catch his ass up. His wife keep reaching out to me. She's definitely a *hello Barbra, this is Shirley* ass bitch. I don't even know how I'm his type. If y'all saw the bitch. I'm baffled." Charles said curling my weave. We both laughed.

"He got kids too?" I asked, and Charles looked at me again through the mirror.

"Bitch, how about I saw him with the Kids. He got a little one no older than three." He shouted. I shook my head and glanced at Tiera typing a mile a minute.

"Boah I swear these niggas and bitches ain't shit." I hissed.

"You hear me." Charles agreed. "I got something for his ass though. He said he had something planned for us tonight. I'mma have her meet us there. Pop out on his weak ass!" Charles clapped and finished curling my weave.

I was in love with the bundles he was now selling and he nailed my closure and curls.

"Alright y'all. Ash, can you get Karson bag together." I asked Ashtyn and she did what was told. I took Karson out Tiera hands and slipped him into his car seat.

"Look, make sure y'all at Ashtyn party tomorrow. Be on time." I told them and paid Charles for my hair and left. I stopped to get my kids something to eat and headed to the hospital.

"Mama Kar, are we going to the hospital?" Ashtyn asked sticking a fry into her mouth.

"Yes love. Are you ready to see mommy?" I replied back. Ashtyn got geeked hopping up and down dancing.

"Yess, but is mommy going to talk to me? I don't want mommy to be tired like last time." she asked and I sighed.

"Mommy is going to be tired but I'm pretty sure she missed you a lot so she's going to talk to you." I told her.

Once we got to the hospital room Ashley was sitting up in bed. When she and Ashtyn's eyes landed on each other you could see the love. They both were so excited to finally see and hug each other. I had to take a picture. It was a heartwarming scene.

"Look mommy, these my brothers and sisters." Ashtyn said getting off the bed pointing to her siblings.

"Nice to finally meet you all." Ashley said. Ashtyn helped Kason get in bed while I turned the TV on and sat the kids up on the couch. I pulled the rolling chair next to Ashley's bed and sat next to her while she held Karson.

"Mommy, I'm so happy you're woke. I have so much to tell you." Ashtyn said clapping her hands together. I laughed at her and leaned back in my seat getting comfortable.

"GIRL, I'm glad they bad asses sleep. They been getting on my nerves!" I told Ashley and she laughed.

"Girl, I been calling yo husband, trying tell him bring my baby to see me." she rolled her eyes and rubbed Ashlyn head. We had been at the hospital chilling for a few hours. Finally the kids tired they self and was knocked out wherever they sat at.

"Yo baby daddy is something else; he on my nerves too!" I told her and she laughed.

"Y'all better take care of my baby. I'm tired of fighting, and I'm tired of struggling." she vented. "I want you to always tell my baby how much I love her and tell her that I'll always be watching her. Just make sure she knows that she's everything to me." Ashley said grabbing my hand. "I'm so hurt, I don't want to leave my baby Karter. I have been calling Jamar because I know I'm dying and I just wanted to see her one last time! She needs me. I need her more! It's killing me more to know that I'm leaving her without me! You gotta love her like she's yours! She is yours. Even if you and Jamar do split. Don't leave my baby!" She told me. When I looked at her, we both had a single tear and she let my hand go. The machines started to go off.

"Ashley... Ashley." I yelled her name waking up Ashtyn.

"Mommy.... No mommy wake up." she instantly started crying. The doctors and nurses walked in and looked at Ashley and checked her pulse. The doctor nodded to the other nurse and she looked at me.

"Do something. Why ain't y'all doing anything?" I yelled feeling myself get emotional.

"I'm sorry. Miss Ashley was a DNR. Do you need me to call anyone to help you with the children?" she asked, and I sighed and shook my head.

Ashtyn was hysterical, and I couldn't even get my other kids under control. I dialed Jamar but he didn't answer. Even after text messages and calling a hundred times. I dialed Jania and she came to help me. On my way home, Ashley cried for her mommy and daddy, but Jamar didn't answer and Ashley was gone. I stopped and got them some pizza on my way home and sat them down for dinner. I couldn't even think straight nor did I have an appetite. I dialed Jamar one last time followed by his niggas in the crew. Nobody answered and I sighed. I dialed Deno, Jamar man on his team and he answered.

"Boss lady?" he answered and I sighed.

"Tell him I said if he doesn't get home in the next twenty minutes his ass won't have a home to come to!" I yelled and threw my phone. It was now one in the morning. The kids were knocked out and I was in bed. I couldn't understand for the life of me what was going on with Jamar. Me and Jamar haven't even had an argument to where we weren't talking and, right now, we couldn't stand each other. I slipped on my robe and house shoes so I could go check on my kids. Mariel and Ashtyn was in Mariel bed together sleep. Jamie was asleep in her own bed. Karson and KJ was asleep in his bed. I went back to my room and tried Jamar one more time, but my call went to voicemail so I called it a night. I would deal with his ass in the morning or whenever he came home.

I felt the bed dip down and smelled Guilty Gucci cologne mixed with Remy Martin liquor. I rolled over to look at my alarm clock and it read 4:34 a.m. I sighed and turned the opposite way and fell back to sleep.

"You know what? FUCK YOU JAMAR! All you worried about is fucking running the streets. YOUR daughter needs you! I fucking needed you!" I yelled getting into his face. This nigga got the fucking nerve to be mad cause I didn't fix him no breakfast this morning. After he came in here the wee hours of the night! He couldn't even call to check on his daughter. That's some whack ass shit for him to walk in here like everything was okay!

"She fucking died in my face! The muthafucka YO ASS

HAD A BABY WITH DIED IN MY FACE!" I yelled feeling the tears drop.

"It ain't the first time you saw a muthafucka die." This dummy said.

Slap.

I couldn't control my anger. When he reached back and acted like he wanted to hit me, all my thoughts went out the window. Little came out of nowhere and shoved Jamar back.

"Man, what the fuck y'all on?" he asked, and I laughed to stop myself from crying.

"You was gone hit me? FUCK YOU JAMAR! I'M DONE! I'm gone!" I yelled going upstairs. I heard the front door shut and went to my room. I grabbed a duffle bag and started to throw clothes in. At this point, if Jamar wanted to move foul, then me and my kids was leaving. FUCK A JAMAR!

14

LITTLE

I was bout to face my fears and go holler at Jania when I pick up the kids. She was finally talking to me.

When I pulled up to the park, I asked Jania could she stick around while I watch the kids play at the park, and surprisingly, she agreed. I played around with the kids for thirty minutes. I didn't want Jania to be restless so I told them to go ahead and play by themselves while I talk to mommy. When I walked up to her car, I felt like a little school boy tryna mack on his crush.

"Can I get inside the car?" I asked her, and I heard her hit the locks so I walked around and got into the passenger seat.

"You wanna tell me how you feel or you want me to start first?" I asked her again.

"You go ahead. I'm listening to you." she said trying to keep it together.

"Okay, look Nini. I know I fucked up and I shouldn't have still been fucking her. She would get me over there to get Ty'Aira and it'll go from there. I'm not putting the blame all on her, though, because she owe you no loyalty. I do. I fucked up big time, and I'm tired of hurting you, man. I miss you. I miss your smile, your smell, waking up next to you in the a.m. and smelling your cooking while I'm getting ready to start my day. Long story short, I want to come home, and I promise to do right this time. On my kids, ma, I don't want her. She's now pregnant and wouldn't get rid of the child. That's my fault, again, but she feels like if she keeps the child I'll come back to her. Even after I told her multiple times I would never leave you for her.

I love you Nini. Please forgive me baby." She didn't say nothing. I could see the tears rolling down her cheeks. I spoke again.

"Please ma. I'll do whatever it takes. Just tell me what I have to do." she cried harder, and I wanted to comfort her, but I knew she'd deny it. I ain't gone lie; it was hurting a nigga heart to know how bad I was hurting her. After a few more minutes, she gained her composure and began to speak.

"Tyree, I love you, too, and what you did hurt me to the core, because you know what I went through with Jason before this, and you still took advantage of me. It won't be easy to forgive you, but I am willing to save my marriage; only way is if you get rid of that baby. You're my husband! And I shouldn't have to share you with her."

"What if she doesn't Nini? I've tried and tried."

"I don't know, Tyree. I can't stand another child. I'm so disgusted with you and her because of that." she told me honestly. I couldn't do nothing but understand, though, cause we was in the wrong anyway.

"She ain't the only one pregnant, Tyree. I'm eight weeks pregnant. And I'm keeping my baby. I shouldn't have to share a pregnancy with your ex-girlfriend. When you get it together let me know what her final decision was. I love you. Call me when the kids are ready to come home. I gotta go." she told me wiping her face and leaning over to kiss my cheek while starting her car up.

"I love you too." I told her getting out the car and calling out to my kids. I watched her as she pulled off, til she was out of sight.

"Y'all ready to go get some dinner?"

"Yes Daddy." T2 said as he struggled to carry his little brother who would be one soon. I grabbed Ty from out of his arms and buckled him into the seat. I texted Tiera to see if I could scoop Ty'Aira for dinner and she said yes. I told her to make sure she'd be dressed and to just send her out when she hear me blowing. She had just started getting her strength back and going to physical therapy while also monitoring the baby weekly to make sure nothing went wrong. She was really excited about the baby even after I told her to get rid of it. She's married and so am I, so I really don't understand why she thought it was okay to keep it like what we doing wasn't wrong enough. I pulled up and hit the horn a couple times and the at-home nurse I hired for her opened the door and watched Ty walk to the car. She opened the front door and hopped in the passenger seat. They decided they wanted seafood so I took them to Red Lobster.

"Daddy, are we all staying at your house tonight?" Ty'Aira asked.

"Yes."

"Good because I missed you and we need to all bond. Just us as in you and your kids." I didn't even respond because she was right. That little girl was so fucking smart it surprised me some days. We spent the rest of our night with dinner and movies while talking about everything under the sun. I missed this and I just wished my wife was here with us. She was the missing piece to our little puzzle.

15

JAMAR

I came home and my wife and kids was gone. Damn was it that bad that I lost what means the most to me? I tried to call Karter phone but it was going straight to voicemail which means she blocked me or turned her phone off. Once I tried a few more times I realized I wasn't going to get anywhere so I walked around the house and started to pick up little things. Before I knew it a few hours had passed and I had cleaned the entire house. That was more than enough time for my wife to return home but still nothing. I called her phone and again I got the voicemail. I thought about calling my family but instead I grabbed my keys and headed out to see whose house I would find her at.

I started at Little crib but she wasn't there so I eventually made my rounds to houses of everyone in our circle. Once I didn't find her I began to get worried. It never dawned on me to call Ashtyn phone to see if she'd answer. I FaceTimed her and she answered on the second ring,

"Hey baby girl."

"Hey daddy, where's Karter?"

"She's in the next room. Her phone is off. We're having

fun daddy so I have to call you back." And she immediately disconnected the call.

Damn, it be your own kids. I knew they were okay, but I didn't know where they were and that's why I was going crazy. I was already out this way so I decided to slide through Head Honcho and have a few drinks to get my mind off my wife and kids. The bartender had always been trying to push up on me, so I'll be sure to fire her when me and my wife is back in touch. I had to run it pass boss lady first.

After my second drink, I immediately started feeling a bad vibe come from her; she was acting very strange and kept looking from me to her phone. I pulled my phone out and texted my crew to fill them in that something was about to go down at the club and to get here immediately. I had Mace already on the cameras to make sure he's watching everything. This dizzy broad had no idea that I was on to her and then I started to feel lightheaded. This bitch must've drugged me but I played it off and asked her to make me another drink. She thought I was paying attention and that's when I seen her putting a substance in my drink. Jania must've been with Little when I texted him because she walked in first and walked up asking for a drink. I noticed as she pulled her gun out and put her silencer on it while she waited for her drink. I watched her put the substance in Jania drink too and turned around like everything was okay.

"Here you are ma'am." Jania chuckled and she spoke again.

"How's your night today?" the bartender Maria asked.

"It was going great. I had to come handle some business. What about yours?" Jania asked back.

"I'm good. Just waiting for the sun to set for me to make some tips, that's all."

"Aw baby girl, you don't have to worry about that. You won't even make it that long."

"Excuse me?" the bartender said unaware that she was about to take her last breathe. Jania shot her once in the foot and she dropped. She walked around the bar and kneeled to her being sure not to make a scene.

"Who are you working for?" Jania asked her.

"What are you talking about? I work for him." She said halfway pointing at me.

"Not anymore." I made clear as I got up and tried to walk but I dropped. Once Jania finished the lil Bitch off she came around to help me.

"Nini call the clean-up crew. Take me home." was the last thing I remember saying before I blacked out.

When I woke up I couldn't even remember what had happened. I was in my room in the bed, and I got up to see if my wife had returned home. I heard movement outside my door so I instantly grabbed my pistol out my nightstand and silently walked to the door. I opened it quickly and had my gun to whoever head it was. Luckily it was just the chef bringing me food.

"Sorry boss. I was just coming to check your temperature and bring you food." She spoke as clear as she could.

"Who else is here?"

"Your family is downstairs sir."

"Sorry about that ma." I said tucking my gun, and I can hear her let out the breath she had been holding. Once I got downstairs all my family was there BUT my wife and kids.

"Ain't nobody talked to my wife?" Everybody in the room shook their head no. "That ain't strange to y'all?"

"It is strange but there's no way for me to contact her.

The phone goes straight to voicemail." Kris spoke up. Everyone agreed once again.

"I called Ashtyn phone and she hung up right in my face. Everything seem okay though." I said walking away to get my phone and try calling her again. This time Karter answered and she was so beautiful.

"Ma where are you?"

"We're out of the country."

"Where tho?"

"We'll be back soon. Bye Jamar." she said and disconnected the call. This shit was blowing me. Jania asked to speak with me alone and she followed me to the backyard. "Brother, whoever these Jamaican fucks is they're really out to get you. Not only is it some Jamaicans, it's a Mexican cartel on our asses too." It all made sense because of Marlon and Selena.

"How you know sis?" I asked rubbing my hand down my face.

"Chick told me she was paid by a Mexican woman and a Jamaican man to drug you and let them know when she was done so they could come kill you." I listened as she continued.

"She said they paid her fifty grand so you know what I did? I made her tell me where it was and then I killed her. She wasn't a liar, though, because the money was exactly where she said it was. I split it twenty-five, twenty-five into our accounts. We gotta handle this ASAP and move around. For the sake of our kids."

"I agree sis. Thank you for being there that day."

"We all was there. I was just the distraction. And you know it's no biggie." Once everybody left the house I turned the camera monitors onto my TV and was calling it a night.

16

KARTER

Jamar had me so fucked up. When I packed up my kids and left, I decided we would come to this little resort in Jamaica, just to show my kids something different. We had been here for the past three days and everything was perfect! I hadn't felt no bad vibes since I got here, and the scenery was amazing. My kids loved it here. The way I was feeling and the way Jamar had been treating us we were gone remain here.

"Come on, guys, let's go." I yelled. I grabbed Karson and our bag. All of us went down the street to the beach.

"Nope. No KJ, don't you dare." I yelled. These kids were getting ready to go right back to the hotel room.

"But mommy I can swim." Kartier told me and I smacked my lips.

"Come down to three feet or don't get in. All of y'all." I told them and they followed me. After taking off my swim-suit cover, I dipped my feet in and picked Karson up.

After about an hour of playing in the pool, I got out with Karson. We sat on the bench and got us a tan as the other kids played.

"Mommy, I don't feel good." Mariel said and laid down on top of me.

"Alright, come on; let's head back to the room. So we can shower and eat." I told them, and we all gathered our things, then went back to the room. After showering and eating, we explored the island and went on a group trip with other tourists to the forest to see some animals. The kids loved that, and we ended our night watching TV and eating popcorn.

The next day, I had to run to the market to get some fruit and just to clear my head. I hesitated on leaving the kids at home but Karson was sleep. I didn't have to worry about hotel staff or other guests snooping around because we stayed at our own vacation house. I knew Ashtyn and Kartier knew how to keep the other two kids in check, so I left them back at the house.

When I entered the market, I was instantly alert. I didn't show it though. I seen a Jamaican, and I understood his broken language more than he thought. I pulled my phone out to text Ashtyn.

The man said, "That's Jamar wife. Marlo baby mama. Should we kill her?"

I knew then exactly who was after my family. I told Ashtyn to get everybody ready, pack as much as they could carry, and be waiting by the back door when I arrived; she had five minutes. She didn't reply but that little girl was so intelligent. I knew she was going to get everything together and do exactly what I said.

I continued to still pick up fruit and finger foods as if I didn't notice them. I also made sure to send Mace a text to have a private jet waiting for us immediately. He sent me the path to take to get to the plane, and I made sure I kept it on my screen. Once I paid for the few items, I walked out of the market and seen the dudes following behind in a car slowly. I had my gun sitting in a drawer inside the house; all I had to do was get to it.

As I went to send Ashtyn the path, a text came through from her saying, "Ready." She was smart like I knew. I told her if I wasn't there in five minutes to follow the path and only let the pilot wait for ten minutes then take off without me. I set the timer for five minutes so that I could keep track of my kids while I tried to get myself to safety. I had about two minutes until I reached the house, and they were still creeping, which means they didn't think I knew they was on to me. My alarm went off which meant that my kids was heading out.

A minute later, I walked in and Ashtyn did such a good job with packing up as much as she could. She even had my things packed up, and I was so thankful. I grabbed a backpack to put the kids' snacks in and my gun. When I got to the back door, I heard whispering, so I took off running up the stairs to go out the back window. I had seven minutes to make it to the plane with my kids. As soon as I hit the window, I heard shooting down below me from the front and back. They thought they had me trapped in with my kids.

When I didn't see anyone below me anymore, I jumped, and when I landed I took off running and never looked back. All I could think about was getting to my children, and the plane was going to take off in three minutes; I was only a minute away. I went running up the stairs onto the plane and all the kids bum rushed me. I hugged every of them one by one and when I got to Ashtyn I hugged her a little longer.

"Thank you, baby girl, you're so brave. I love you so much."

"I love you too." We hugged again as we got seated,

because we felt the plane starting to take off. We all bundled up next to each other. My adrenaline was rushing so I knew I wasn't getting no sleep. I just watched my children start to doze off, and I silently thanked the man above for letting us make it back home. I sent Jamar a text letting him know we needed to talk immediately when I got home. He replied and said he loved us and couldn't wait to see us. I chuckled a little bit to myself, because I'm already knowing this nigga was going crazy those little couple days we was gone.

17

CHARLES

Looking in the mirror, my appearance wasn't bad. I mean, I was a handsome ass nigga. My dark skinned complexion glistened under the light, and my fresh haircut and line-up was perfect. My smile was perfect, and my pearly whites made it that way. I wasn't fat. Matter of fact, I was cocky and fit as hell. On the outside, I seemed perfect, but on the inside, I was broken.

Every relationship I have been in just wasn't meant to be. I can't even lie, this shit with Lance crushed me. Put me on a whole other level. Everybody around me think I'm strong and not supposed to have feelings, but that's far from me! I want to love like everybody else. I want a happily ever after. From the very beginning, I was trained to kill, but because of all the killing I done did, this was my karma.

I had my music on while I was getting dressed. Today I was rocking a short-sleeve, white and gold Versace button up, with some white Versace Skinny Jeans. On my feet was, of course, the gold Versace loafers. I made sure my jewelry was on froze. I sprayed my Gucci Guilty on and grabbed my jacket. I made sure my pistols was on each side of me and left out. Today, I decided to drive my all-white twenty twenty-four costume made Jeep. I was applying all pressure just to show this weak ass nigga what his biggest blessing was!

After texting Morrisa, Lance's wife asking what's the address, I hopped on the highway. Today, we were finally getting his ass. I'm surprised he didn't get the hint. His trifling ass been calling and texting, blowing me up, but I would just ignore him. I told him I wanted to talk, and that I would text him at the restaurant of my choice. The fact that this slow ass girl decided to meet at some fucking Golden Coral all you can eat buffet was beyond me! I mean, don't get me wrong, Golden Corral got some fire ass rolls, but an all you can eat buffet? Come on, now, sis! I had on my Sunday's best! She could have at least picked Benihana.

When I pulled up, I parked and walked in. I saw Morrisa sitting at the back table just eating like it was nothing. This bitch was so nonchalant her ass was used to this. That's what made it sick! I wasn't used to these type of games! That's why that nigga was gone have to see me! I sat down and she smiled.

"Glad you finally could do this. Tired of this nigga walking around like he ain't living foul." she said and I nodded.

"I mean, you already said I'm not the first guy. So how many has it been?" I asked.

I don't know why I wanted answers. I guess for closure, but nothing she or his ass could say would ease the pain.

"Only three... How long? You know have y'all been together?" She asked, and I rolled my eyes.

"Girl, eight fucking years... Never got any indication that he was cheating or any of that." I told her and she nodded.

"He's a bad ass boah, I tell you that. I don't know how long he's been cheating. I just found out... Maybe about five years ago.... You the longest one he ever had around. You gotta be special." She said, and I wanted to punch the bitch lights out. I mean, she gotta be some type of special. I just shut my mouth and didn't speak back to Morrisa. She was annoying me with the questions, and I refused to look even more stupid asking questions. After I texted Lance with my location, he came scrolling in with a bouquet of flowers. He must not have noticed Morrisa cause he kept walking towards me and even kissed my cheek.

"Hey babe. I missed you. You ain't been fucking with ya mans?" he asked. He walked to the other side of the table then stopped dead in his tracks once he noticed Morrisa sitting across from me.

"Hello to you also hubby." she smiled sipping her drink.

"What are you doing here man?" he asked her, and I laughed.

"So this is yo wife right?" I asked pushing my chair back. I had to count to ten because these people want to see me act a donkey.

"Man, let me explain." He tried to plead but Morrisa laughed.

"Please just tell this faggot so we can go Lance." This bold ass bitch said.

"Tell me... Please tell me!" I said wondering.

"Look, I'mma tell you. He was only hired to kill you and take out yo brothers! Shit, he just fell in love with yo ass." she sassed slamming her cup down.

"You was plotting?" I asked, hurt dripping from my voice. I mean, hearing that, my heart shattered. Not only was he a lying, cheating bastard, but he was the enemy!

"Man, let me ex...."

"Nah boo, tell him. C... Charles, whatever yo name is. My nigga was only hired to take you out, that's it! So now you can tread lightly! Cause we coming for y'all. Every last one of y'all." she taunted and stood up. So did I.

"Listen and listen good. He knows he messed up. That's why he ain't saying nothing. And for what you just said out your mouth, you will die. So go tell yo kids goodbye. If I was y'all, I would run. Because I'm coming, and I'm coming full throttle." I hissed and walked away. Every step I took my heart turned cold. When I got in my car, I called Jock on the verge of tears.

"Wassup? Jamar answered on the first ring.

"Jamar. I need you right now."

"You crying man?" He asked.

"Shit almost."

"Pull up to the crib." he told me and disconnected the call. I was in shock cause he already knew it was Lance bullshit. Jamar was the closest thing I had. Ever since we were little we just became super close. That was my boy, and I knew if nobody had an open ear and arms he would.

When I got there, he was chilling, smoking a blunt in his front room. He looked like he needed to vent himself.

"Wassup? Who hurt yo feelings man? That weird ass nigga Lance?" He got straight to the point.

"Yes, I'm killing him. I already told him say his last goodbyes to his kids. because his time on earth has expired. I'm in my feelings tonight but tomorrow, it's on!"

"What exactly happened though." Jamar asked.

"You know we been steady these last four years. Come to find out this man got a wife, kids, all that. How could I not know? And the sickest part about it all is that the wife knew he slept with men. Ain't this some shit?" I wondered to myself.

"Yeah, the sickest shit at that."

"That's not even the killer part cous," I stopped to hit the blunt. "This nigga said he was only with me for four years because he was supposed to kill me."

"Kill you?"

"Yeah, for the same cats."

"These damn Jamaicans ain't gone get enough." Jamar stated matter of factly.

"It's a lot of them motherfuckers, but our team so strong we can get every single last one of them. Shit, me and you by our self can." He continued to say. Before I could respond, Karter and the kids came bursting in the front door.

"Baby!" Jamar sounded so excited. All the kids ran into his arms, and it was so heartwarming to see. He kissed every single last one of them and told them he loved them all.

"Okay guys, it's late. Go get ready for bed, and me and daddy will be up to tuck y'all in." Karter told them, and they all went up the stairs.

"Hi CiCi." she said kissing my cheek.

"I'm glad both of y'all here, because y'all not gone like what I'm about to tell y'all."

"Kick it to me sis." I told her.

"So you know Jamar pissed me off right? I decided to go down to this little resort in Jamaica."

"Aw shit." I said.

"Let her finish cous." Jamar butted in.

"So we chilling for two days, having the time of our lives. This morning, I wake up and head to the market. I left the kids at the house by themselves. As I'm in the market, I felt the stares and then I heard the whispers. They referred to me as your wife but Jamar baby momma, and they said they was gone kill me. All I could think about was my kids so I continued to play it off right?

So boom, I pull out my phone and text Ashtyn. Jamar, that girl is so smart and brave. She amazed me ,and after today I know that girl will do anything for her brothers and sisters. But back to the story, so I text her, right, and I tell her pack your sisters and brothers up and get as much stuff as we can carry and you got five minutes. I didn't receive a text back so I'm nervous thinking about our safety. I texted Mace and told him get us a jet immediately cause we had to get out of there. I bought some fruit and snacks just to continue to play it off as if I didn't see them.

As I'm at the register getting ready to send Ashtyn the path to get to the jet, she texted a simple ass ready. I told her follow the path, and if I'm not there ten minutes after they get settled then to leave me. I gets home, and she done packed up everything so good, even my shit. So, I grabbed my gun and put the snacks into a book bag and head towards the back door. I heard whispering which means they had surrounded the house that quick. I found an escape and they lit that whole house up. I made it to the plane within a minute before they were supposed to leave, and I was so thankful for Ashtyn. These Jamaican bitches gotta go. They done crossed the line." She finally finished with her story.

"Sis, Lance told me he only been with me this long because he was paid to kill me by some Jamaican niggas." I told her.

"It's all starting to make sense now. And I'm ready for war; it's one thing to fuck with my family but you done involved my kids."

"I agree." I said. Whole time, Jamar is in his thoughts; he ain't said a word. He got up and walked over to her and kissed her ass so passionately it made me think about Lance ass.

"Bro, kill that nigga." Jamar told me and I nodded. What a day this has been. I know one thing for sure and two for certain. These bitches done fucked with the wrong family. Everybody wanted the ruthless C. Well, here he goes!

18

KARTER

I was so glad to be back home. The kids went to bed but I knew they would be up bright and early because they didn't eat dinner, just the snacks I had bought. I had showered and was ready to sleep comfortably in own bed in my own home. Once I moisturized my body, I went to climb into bed. Jamar instantly pulled me into him, and I was expecting an argument but that didn't happen.

"I missed you baby. I apologize for leaving the way I did, but you had me fucked up."

"It's okay, ma. I'm just so happy y'all back home and safe. Don't do that dumb shit again." He told me as he climbed between my legs and started to devour my pussy. Oh how I've missed this shit. It took no time for him to make me cum. He came up and kissed my lips, and I loved when he did that because I loved to taste myself.

"Give me all of you." I told him and he wasted no time sliding in me. "Ah, fuck Jamar."

"I'm just listening to your instructions." His smart ass said. He made me feel every inch, literally, as he gave me deep, long strokes.

"I love you Karter." He told me.

"I love you more bae." I told him pulling him down for a kiss. For the rest of the night, we made love to each other, and it just reminded me why I loved this man so damn much. At about 5:45am, I woke up to my phone ringing off the hook. I picked it up off the nightstand and called out to Jamar.

"Who is it?" He asked with his eyes still closed.

"It's a private call."

"Answer." And I did as told.

"Next time you won't be able to escape bitch." The man on the other end said in his broken English then disconnected the call.

"Lay back down bae; we not worried about them."

It just wasn't meant for me to sleep because by seven o'clock the kids were waking up for breakfast which I expected. I got up and made everyone breakfast which consisted of sausage, eggs, pancakes and apple juice. On my way back upstairs to handle Karson, I walked into Jamar already changing his diaper.

"Hi daddy man. Where you been man." I listened to him say as he picked him up and kissed him. "Thank you so much Karter. I can't express how much y'all have changed my life."

"We love you, bae. You don't have anything to worry about. We stuck together."

"Yeah, til death do us part. That's the only way you getting away from me."

"Vice versa." I said walking out the room and going to my room to get back in bed.

I laid there thinking about my life as I dozed off again. Bitches would kill to be in my shoes. We weren't perfect but damn sure close to it. I had the ring, the babies, the house, and the money all without trying. As my eyes shut, I got another private, missed call, which I chose not to answer. I silenced my phone and turned over to get comfortable and go back to sleep.

Getting up the next morning, the kids and Jamar was gone so I decided to go see C and get my hair done, but he told me the shop was closed for the day. He also told me what was going on with Lance and I felt for him. He was so lovable and loving. He didn't deserve to get his heart broken by men that wasn't ready to come out the closet or just flat out didn't want him. He promised he would get me in tomorrow, and we disconnected the call. After fixing myself breakfast, I sat at the table eating. I called Jamar but he didn't answer.

"Hello Mrs. Karter." Christa, the chef/maid, greeted coming into the kitchen. She had the dirty clothes hamper taking it downstairs to the laundry.

"It's fine. I can do the laundry." I told her reaching for the basket.

"Are you sure? I don't mind." Christa asked, and I nodded.

"It's okay Christa. Go relax." I told her and took the basket downstairs. Separating the clothes first I started to put the dark clothes in the washer first. I went through all the pockets, because Jamar always kept money, jewelry, shit anything in his pockets. After putting all the clothes in and starting the washer, I headed to his office. The door was unlocked so I went in. The computer was off, but it was a folder on top of it. I didn't look in it, but everything was telling me to look inside. I declined and snooped around to see what else I could see out of place. I wasn't trying to be nosey, but my husband had been moving real weird lately and, if he was cheating or had someone else I wanted to know! Finding nothing I went back to my bedroom and got in the shower. Stepping out, I dried my body then oiled it down. Stepping into some red lace panties, I slipped on some light denim skinny jeans with rips in them. Jamar came walking into the room with a sleeping Karson in his arms.

"Hey I called you." I said. I tried to kiss him on the cheek but he curved me, making me laugh. "Oh. Okay." I said. Slipping on a white Chanel tank top I slipped on my Chanel slides and tied my hair into a ponytail.

"Hey, where did y'all go?" I asked and he didn't respond. He just ignored me and sat on the bed. I went to my dresser and put on a diamond watch, matching necklace and earrings.

"Hey, well I'm going to the grocery store. Text me if you want anything." I said and he nodded.

"Take security with you." he yelled once I stomped out the room. I guess he was back to being Jamar that I knew these past few months.

19

TIERA

I was back on my feet with the help of physical therapy within two weeks. I still had slight pain sometimes but it wasn't nothing I couldn't handle. Everything was healing well. So I was hitting the streets today.. I was having lunch with Little today, and I'm sure he wanted to talk about this baby situation. I didn't want to get rid of my baby. I loved Tyree. and he needed to come home where he's supposed to be. I

had to start getting ready early since I moved so slow with these casts. I couldn't wear something sexy to draw his attention so I decided on a real cute and comfortable PINK blue and yellow outfit with the Laney retro fives. My Lyft pulled up exactly thirty minutes after I finished getting dressed, perfect timing. We decided we would meet at Ruth Chris because a New York strip sounded amazing. and that was both of our favorites. I was long overdue for a good meal. because the hospital food got old quick! As soon as I was seated. I asked for a glass of Moscato so that I could sip my wine and wait on this man. He walked in looking like the sexy chocolate nigga that he is. Lord, I needed to change my panties immediately. He sat down and got straight to the point, which means he must've been trying to make up to his Bitch. I rolled my eyes to clearly show I was irritated.

"So wassup? What you gonna do about the baby?" he said.

"Hello to you, too, asshole, and I'm keeping my baby. I made that clear to you and your bitch."

"I don't want another baby Tiera." he told me.

"Well, too bad Tyree. You shouldn't have been fucking me." He blew out his breath as he rubbed his hand down his face.

"Alright man, do you." He said getting up.

"Where are you going Little?" I asked, curious to know because we hadn't even started lunch yet.

"I ain't come here for this and just to avoid any conflict I'mma leave. I'll bang yo line later when it's time for me to get Ty'Aira." And with that, he walked away and out of the restaurant. I was so embarrassed. I'm already crippled. Now I'm lonely and crippled.

When I walked into my mama house, my mood went from bad to worst. I didn't even notice the extra car in the driveway. I groaned and walked around the corner anyways.

"Hey ma..." I greeted and she smiled and stood up.

"Hey Tiera. Little just left from getting the kids." she spoke and looked back. I looked around her and instantly got heated. His little bitch was sitting there all perfect and glowing.

"I'm glad you here because I wanted you two to speak." My mother said.

"I don't got shit to say to her!" I snapped getting ready to turn to leave.

"Look, I just wanna say one thing." Jania said standing

up. I rolled my eyes and laughed. I knew she was glowing for a reason, and that little pudge gave it all away.

"I'mma let y'all talk." My slow ass mama said and left. "Whatever you and Tyree had going on is over Tiera. I'm his WIFE. I'm who he WANTS to be with. We have 2 children and one on the way. He's not going anywhere and neither am I. You can have that little baby or whatever, and he's going to do what he have to do to take care of his kids with you but other than that, all that other shit is done with!" she said and shifted her weight to the other foot. I laughed a little bit from stopping myself from smacking the shit out of her.

"Listen boo. Little and I have been doing this since we was kids! We have years invested! I'm having his child and, like he said earlier at breakfast, we are gone work on getting back together." I lied while smiling in her face.

"I know y'all got years invested but have you ever got a ring? No. Cause I'm wife bitch and will forever be! I don't give a fuck how many years and kids y'all have invested! I have that nigga whole heart! And he'll cut YOU off if I tell him too! So text him and tell him thank you for getting you pregnant cause if it wasn't for my step child in yo stomach I would've beat yo ass! Now let me get going. MY man wants to take Me and our kids shopping." she said and grabbed her purse, but not before bumping me on her way out.

I groaned in frustration and turned and left right after. Little could play these games all he wanted, but when I got through with her ass he won't have no choice but to come crawling back to me.

When I got in my Uber my phone started to ring.

"Thank you for waiting. You can take me home." I told the guy and he nodded.

"Hello?" I yelled once my phone started to annoy me from ringing too much.

"Leave that girl alone! Tiera, you cause enough fucking problems!" my mother said and I hung up in her face. Fuck her, too, if she wasn't riding with me! When my Uber pulled up at home, my mood had went from worst to fucking hell! Markel was sitting on the steps, waiting on me, looking lost as hell. I groaned and grabbed my purse. I tipped the Uber good. Markel came rushing to help me once he realized I was getting out the Uber. I rolled my eyes and walked past him.

"We need to talk." he insisted and I groaned.

"Look, not right now. I have a bad migraine." I said unlocking my door. I walked in and he walked in after me.

"So you having this nigga baby?" he asked and I sighed. "So how you know it ain't mine." He asked. I slammed my purse and keys down on the table and sat down. I was praying he didn't get on this bullshit. It's not even a possibility that he could be the father. Matter of fact, shit, I was certain he wasn't the daddy. This baby was Little's and I said what I said!

"I know it's not yours cause I got pregnant two weeks after the last time we did it. Markel, I keep telling you that!" I hissed.

"I'm not trying to make you mad. You just hurt me, ma. You been fucking that nigga the whole time?" his crybaby ass whined.

"Me and Little is together now. If you don't like it take it up with him. He's on his way so you need to leave," I stated and he turned away and left. I locked the doors and went to the kitchen to fix myself something to eat. I had to start planning on how I was getting this bitch out the picture.

20

KRIS

"I'm living my best life. Ain't going back and forth with you niggas." I sang as I whipped my car through traffic.

Friday afternoon, and everybody was rushing home to start the weekend. Not me, though. I was rushing to my lawyer's office, because Brandon finally decided he wanted to sit down and talk. Of course since we're going thru the divorce, I told him to meet me downtown. Ever since we split, my whole life went from shitty to great. I was now in a different head space. Didn't have to worry about dodging bullets, because I spent less time with the family. Everything was fine with me though.

Since the house I was staying in with Brandon was his, me and my children packed and left. After staying in a hotel for a week, my mama hooked me up with a friend of hers and got me a nice little four bedroom house in a nice, White neighborhood. I ain't worked a day in my life so Bran thought I was gone be assed out. This nigga was being petty. Had my car repossessed and emptied my bank account that he opened for me. I wasn't tripping, though. Little did he know I was set for life.

Brandon kept my pockets laced the whole six years. So every time he cashed out on shopping sprees and "I'm sorry" money and laced my bank account up, all I did was take out a little at a time and set it aside in a private account he knew nothing about. He thought him taking my car was something, but I copped me something bigger and better. He thought emptying my bank account put a dent in my pocket, but nigga I been moving the money out the account. Who was he trying to play and this dummy didn't have a prenup... So guess who was paying for all my lawyer fees? Him.

I didn't want anything though. Child support and that's it! Everything else, I was fine leaving without. As long as he signed the papers and paid child support. When I stepped out my brand new red Rolls Royce Cullinan SUV all eyes was on me. I was feeling myself. My short hairstyle was replaced with a wavy 30-inch weave, courtesy of my boo Ci. He had my makeup and lashes nailed. I was rocking a white Gucci blouse, with the red and blue Gucci design on the collar and cuffs. I had on the matching slacks with some red Louis Vuitton Heels. I had on light jewelry and a matching Louis Bag. I had to show this nigga what he was missing! If he couldn't do right by me and my three then somebody else will. I hit the lock on my key chain and walked into the building, as my lawyer was walking in also.

"Hello Ms. Kris. Thank you for being on time today. How is your evening?" Chandler James asked me as we shook hands.

"It's been good so far. How are you today?" I asked and he opened the door for me as we entered the meeting room.

"It's been okay... Better now that I get to be in your presence." He winked and I laughed.

"Yeah, you must say that to all yo clients." I asked, and he winked pulling the papers out his briefcase.

"Your husband isn't trying to sign those papers." he told me and I sighed. "I see why. If my wife look like you she wouldn't be able to get rid of me either," he flirted and I giggled.

"Well, good thing you aren't my husband. So what did he call me here for, if he not trying..." the door swung open, and Brandon and his lawyer walked in. He looked at me in pure disgust and I smiled.

"Hello James. Hello Jackson." his lawyer spoke to me and Chandler.

"Hey." I dryly replied.

"Okay. I was telling my client that you refused to sign the papers. I'm not sure if you are asking..."

"Look man. I don't want a divorce. I'm asking for whatever you need me to do, I'll do it." Brandon said cutting Chandler off. "Ma, I fucked up. And I'll go to rehab, I'll get out the streets. I'll do whatever you need me to do. I don't wanna lose you and my seeds." Brandon begged and I shook my head.

"Just sign the papers Brandon." I yelled and stood up. "I'm done here. If any more questions take it up with my lawyer." I voiced and walked out.

When I got into my car, I dialed my mother's number; she didn't answer so I headed towards her house. Karter was pulling up, and we both got out of the car at the same time.

"Hey sis?" She sang hugging me. I used my key to unlock the door. Janet was laying on the couch with my brothers Mace and Mason.

"Well, it was nice to invite us to the party." I said. Janet smiled and scooted over so we could sit.

"Well, this a once-in-a-lifetime thing. Got all my babies here under one roof." She said and Mace laughed.

"Take advantage man; take advantage." he joked imitating Chris Rock off *Friday* the movie.

"What's going on with y'all?" My mother asked and Karter shrugged.

"Well, you wasn't answering so I stopped by......" I told her and she looked under the pillow for her phone.

"My phone was on silent."

"Bran and I also went to meet up with our lawyers." I told her biting my bottom lip.

"Well, let me get out of here." Mace said standing up.

"I gotta go get Bria from work." he said and hugged us.

"I'mma ride with him." Mason said, and they both left out.

"So how did that go?" Karter pulled a bottle of Patron out her purse and sighed. "I'm going through some stuff too, so we might as well have some sips." she said and I agreed.

"Okay, so what did he say about the divorce?" Janet asked.

"Boah, he talking about he don't want a divorce and this and that. Then said he'll do whatever I need." I replied back looking at her. "I didn't want to hear it though. I just left. I don't have time for the stuff. I just want him to sign the papers and that's it." I told them.

"So it's nothing he can do to......" My mother started to ask, and I shook my head.

"Nope! Nothing at all like maybe if he gets rehab, counseling and then maybe. Just maybe. " I told her straight up.

"So how is the kids doing with all this?" Karter asked texting on her phone.

"To be honest. They just going with the flow. They be over Eva house so much, then in between Brandon and my house. It's no time to actually sit them down and ask." I told her. "I do have a friend." I told them smiling.

"Unt-unt. Not a good idea with all this stuff going on to bring somebody new in the picture." Karter told me.

"And why not?" I asked.

"Kris, it's a lot going on within the family and shit. You going through the divorce. It's just not smart." Karter said and I rolled my eyes.

"Sorry sis, we wouldn't be in this shit if it wouldn't be for your weak ass baby daddy!" I said.

"Girl, fuck you! Did you forget I did what the fuck I had to do! Or did you forget I did that shit because of what he did to you!" She shouted standing up. I knew Karter was battling some issues when it came to killing Marlo and Selena. It was a touchy subject but her bringing up what I did in my spare time was none of her business!

"Okay, and you did what you had to do, cause the bitch took your son, not because of me! Fuck you! Only reason we all going thru this shit is cause you brought this fucked up ass nigga in our life!" I yelled standing up too! My sister and I never fought ever. The way I'm feeling she could definitely catch these hands like a bitch on the streets.

"Girl, don't blame ME for yo marriage failing! It's yo own fault you push away every nigga you be with! It ain't my fault you can't keep a man!" she yelled going toe to toe with me.

"Sit the fuck down! Both of y'all!" Janet screamed standing between us.

"Nah fuck her! She want smoke with me so bad!" Karter yelled.

"Fuck you Karter!" I yelled back grabbing my purse off the couch and storming out.

21

BRANDON

"Look, we gotta get this shit packed and shipped!" I yelled to my crew. "Fuck this up and I can dispose of every last one of y'all. It's nothing to get new niggas that want it just as y'all but maybe even more!" I shouted. I blew my nose in the tissue and rubbed it. It became a habit to rub my nose every time I talked.

"You catching a cold Big B?" one of the niggas snickered and then whispered to his homeboy. I laughed and stood up.

"Come here....... you come here and you too." I pointed out to him and his friends. They approached and I laughed.

"What did you say?" I asked and soon as the dude opened his mouth, I shot em in the head. He dropped and I bent down.

"Bro what you say? I ain't hear you?" I asked and he said nothing. I heard water dripping and looked up; his friend was pissing on himself.

"This nigga!" I laughed and shot him in the head.

"Do anybody else got something to say?" It was silent.

"Clean this shit up and let's get to work." I yelled and

went to the back to start helping these slow ass niggas with shipping our product out.

"Look, this what we gonna do. When we go there we ain't asking no questions. We just gone start shooting." Charles said and I nodded.

"Man, what's going on with you? You been moving real reckless lately." Little asked Charles and he sighed.

I looked at Jamar in the back seat, and he was texting away on his phone. I sighed and pulled my phone out thinking about sending Kris a text. I know I fucked up big time with her; I missed her crazy ass. It ain't no going back though. She wasn't fucking with me, and I don't blame her. My own aunty wasn't fucking with me, and to be honest, the shit was getting to me.

"Man, come on; let's just run up in this bitch." I gassed Charles up. Charles was always the thinker of us. He was a trained killer so I was following him.

"Alright bet." Jamar said still looking at his phone. Charles was already pulling his Glock out and cocking it back.

"Man, come on; y'all niggas not thinking." Little said.

"We don't know how many people in that bitch! Them niggas might be hundred deep!" Little said and I laughed.

"When has that ever stopped us nigga." Charles voiced hopping out of the car.

Charles was on great bullshit now. I can see it. That was my nigga so I was on whatever he was. I hopped out, too, and Jamar followed then Little. Charles and I went to the front while Jamar and Little went to the back. I kicked the door down, and Charles marched in right after, squeezing his trigger. I followed his lead, lighting up anything and everything that moved.

"Get that nigga. Get em!" I heard Jamar yell. Creeping towards the back of the house, a nigga ran right past me, but I was on his ass popping him in the leg first. When he fell he turned over shooting. Charles grabbed me, dodging behind the wall. Charles aimed and shot once and no more gunfire was heard.

"Fuck man." Jamar yelled and him and Little came walking towards the front with us. Jamar grabbed the dude who was running and hit em. The dude eyes popped open and I laughed.

"This nigga man." I said, and Little and Jamar grabbed him. Little threw him the chair and Jamar sat across. I just stood there for dramatic effects. My mind kept wandering back to Kris and my daughters, and I cringed at the fact that she was really divorcing me. Wasn't nothing I could do about it. My lawyer said, all I need to do is sign the papers before she started to say she wanted half of everything I had. Knowing Kris she wouldn't do that. She didn't even put up a fight when I got my car I bought her back. She went and upgraded, bounced back like nothing happened.

"Wo erè gwo fukin erè" he sang out and Jamar looked at me.

"I don't know what the fuck you saying but you better speak English before I blow yo head off!" Charles roared and kicked the nigga backwards. Little picked him up and sighed.

"You got about two minutes before you be like the rest of yo people." Jamar told him and inched closer to him.

"English muthafucka!" I yelled and slapped him with the pistol. He spit out blood and winked at me.

"SEE YOU IN HELL PUSSY!" he sang and laughed.

Jamar stood up and emptied the clip into his head. Little and I ran around the house trying to find anything we could while Jamar and Charles trashed and torched it. When I got to the back room, I found folders and pictures. It was pictures of the families and maps of shit. I grabbed all the papers I could and we got the hell out of dodge, but not before making sure the house went up in flames. We all decided to head to the strip club to get some drinks and just relax. Ducking off in VIP I saw one of the little females I got caught up with. She waved at me and decided to come to VIP. I don't know why I wasn't fucking with her or no other chick for that matter. I was trying to get in good with wifey again, and I couldn't have distractions fucking that up.

"You good Bran?" Charles asked and I nodded.

"Yeah, I'm chillin bro. How you been though? You good?" I asked and he shrugged.

"Just ready for all this shit to be over with. We have been in the game too long for us to be getting stood on like this." he told me over the music and I agreed. "We gone get it together! Then take our family on vacation. We gon get it right." he said and I leaned back sipping my drink as Jamar and Little thru cash on the strippers. These bitches wasn't getting a dime out of me!

When I pulled up to Kris house, all the lights were off inside so I knew everybody was asleep. I waited for a second and called her phone. She didn't answer so I leaned my seat all the way back and cut my car off. This was my routine every day. She ain't know but I would sleep out here in my car just to feel close to them and be gone by the time she was up in the morning. I needed to make amends with my wife, because soon, I wouldn't be here to make shit right. I felt it.

22

LITTLE

"Look shorty. I'm trying spend time with my wife. You told me to bring Ty'aira home, I did that!" I said into the phone.

"I don't give a fuck! I asked you could you take me to the hospital because I wasn't feeling good and been having pains! So you telling me yo ugly ass wife is more important than our seed?" Tiera Delusional ass yelled on the other side of the phone.

"Bitch, call the fucking ambulance if it's that deep! All this fucking time you been arguing with me you could've been on yo way to the hospital!" I yelled into the phone. Jania snatched the phone and put it up to her ear.

"Hey Tiera... this Jania. Listen, if you want us to come take you to the hospital we on our way...... Okay... well you said you wanted.... Okay, well any other questions you can call my phone. I'm cutting my husband's phone off...... I know you have my number. You just text me last night. Mhm, okay girl, bye now." Jania said and hung up. "She's bitter." Jania laughed and I shook my head.

When I say this bitch was trying make my life a living

hell. I thought niggas was tripping when I used to hear about the bitter baby mama shit they was going threw. I believe that shit now. I had a baby mama picked first class from hell. I didn't deserve that shit! I was a good ass daddy to my seeds! Shit better than the daddy I had, I know that. I sighed and we pulled up into the shopping outlet.

"It's gonna be okay baby. Don't let her stress you out." Jania said and kissed my cheek. She grabbed her purse and hopped out. So did I. Ever since we been back on track everything been going smoothly. Jania been taking this Tiera shit well. I'm surprised too! I just know once Ti have this baby Jania gone drag her ass. Her words, not mine.

"Okay, so I was thinking bout the house we saw yesterday." she said and smirked

"I knew you was gone pick that one." I told and she laughed.

"I just feel like if it was secluded enough then it would be perfect. We will be having too much shit going on to have neighbors." she told me and I agreed.

"It's so hard to find a house." she sighed dragging out the D on hard.

"I just want us to find a nice 4 to 5 bedroom, 2 story, built-in pool, theatre room, 4 -5 bathroom house. Dang is it that hard." she pouted and I laughed.

"Yeah, we been looking since how long? Two months! We might as well settle on the one we saw." I tested, and she looked at me rolling her eyes.

"Bae, now why would we settle? We not in a rush to move. Even though I would love to have Ty birthday at our new spot." she wondered as we went into the store.

"Bae this cute?" Jania asked holding up a dress. I nodded not really paying attention but paying attention to the nigga and chick that had been following us to the 3rd store. I shook my head and sighed. I was sick of this shit. The last time I had to look over my shoulder was when I was hustling on the streets. Yeah, a long ass time ago...

"I'm really just gone go 'head on and get this." Jania said and sat down by me. "I don't know if you paying attention but they been following us since we came in the mall." Jania told me and kissed my cheek. She stood up and so did I. After we paid for the stuff, we started to walk towards the entrance. When we got into the stairwell of the shopping mall, Jania went first and I stayed behind the door. When the girl and dude came out the same door, they both pulled they guns out, and I came from behind the door as it closed and pulled both my straps out."

"Drop em." I said and put both my guns to they head.

"Fuck!" The chick hissed, and Jania came up the stairs with her gun on both of them.

"Don't try nothing stupid and get y'all ass blasted!" Jania roared, and they both handed they guns over to her.

"Walk!" I pushed them with guns in the back of they head. They walked. "Pull right there." I instructed Jania as she pulled into the warehouse parking lot. She got out the car first and opened the passenger's side back door, and the dude got out first then I got out and instructed the girl to get out. When we got inside, Jamar and Brandon was already inside. Jania kissed me goodbye and left. I sent her to go over Charles, cause he hasn't been answering the phone in a few days for me... Or nobody for that matter. Brandon and I tied the couple up, and I started with the dude first. Dude looked like he would talk before the chick. I pulled a chair right in front of dude and cocked my pistol back.

"I'mma ask you one time and one time ONLY. Who sent you?" I asked, and he looked at chick.

"Man, don't look at her. She can't save you...... Only you

can... You can walk out of here or die." I taunted. Either way he was dying. I just wanted him to think he had an option.

"Boo, don't say shit..." Jamar shot her straight in the head, and the dude screamed out.

"Nooooooo." he cried.

"So what's it gone be?" I asked and leaned backwards.

"We weren't gonna kill you. We only wanted her. We was hired to take out her and only her. Leave you be. But we knew you weren't gonna let us just kill her, so we were just gone kill her once we knew you were at the mall. We were supposed to snatch her when she was left alone. Please don't kill me! I got sons!" he cried out. It was too late, though; he made his choice on living or drying when he tried me and my girl. I shook my head and sighed.

"Man who hired you bro?" I asked, and he looked at Jamar and then at me.

"His sister."

23

JANET

"Hey Miss Jackson. How is your morning?" My coworker Lisa asked.

"It's going well...... Until I walked into this muthafucka." I said to myself. I clocked in and grabbed my patient sheet. Being head nurse in my hospital was exhausting, but I loved my job. I have been a nurse since I was eighteen, and now I'm forty-five years young. The alarm started going, and the blue lights started to flash.

"Door two. Door two." I yelled to my workers as I rushed to the door.... The EMTs pushed the victim in.

"Shot victim, in and out of conscious. Two bullets to the lower torso and one to the back," he rattled off and I slipped the breathing machine on his mouth. I cut his shirt open and started to cut his pants off.

"Page Doctor Wilson, looks like we are losing him. We're going to operation room four." I told them and rushed to the operating room. When we got the victim there, the doctors was already there waiting. I helped transfer the body to the O.R. table and proceeded to help the doctor on what they needed me to do.

"You are truly blessed to be alive Mr. Langston." I told my patient and continued to write in my charts.

"Call me Tony. Don't I know that. I'm getting too old for this shit." he said and laughed.

"On a scale from one to ten, ten being the worst. What's your pain level?" I asked and checked his breathing and blood pressure.

"Eight." He groaned as I lifted his hand.

"I know they told me you turned down the pain meds earlier. Would you like some now?" I asked and he sighed...

"I been clean for seven years. I don't want to-," He proudly started to say.

"Hey no, it's fine. I understand." I cut him off and pat his arm. "You strong. You can get thru this." I told him and finished doing what I needed to do. After checking on all the rest of my patients for the day, I went to my desk.

It was going on at seven in the morning, and I was going to breakfast. I dialed Kris.

"Hey hello?" she answered.

"Good morning. What are you doing?" I asked and she sighed.

"Nothing, just dropped the kids off to Bran. Bored." she responded.

"Well, call Karter. She probably ain't doing nothing." I told her, and she smacked her lips.

"Ma, I'm not calling her, period, and I don't wanna talk to her either!" Kris hissed and I sighed.

"Y'all acting like some little ass kids. Sisters argue every day and be right back talking to each other the same day!" I told her, and she smacked her lips again.

"It don't matter. I'm not." She responded.

"Girl, who are you talking to?" I asked her. She smacked her lips again and sighed.

"Please smack those lips again, so I can smack you." I warned and she sighed.

"Momma. I just don't wanna talk to her okay?" she replied, and this time I smacked my lips.

"Girl, you the oldest. Call yo sister now." I told her and hung up the phone. After I went to get my breakfast from a local spot down the way, I went back to the hospital and ate in the cafeteria. On my way to clock back in, Kris called me.

"You happy now?" she asked soon as I answered.

"Yes I am." I smirked and she laughed.

"You kill me. What you doing anyways?" she asked.

"I'm clocking back in girl... tired!" I told Kris.

"Ma, you have been working a lot. We all just been going through so much; we need a getaway." Kris vented and I agreed.

"Definitely do.... but let me get off this phone. I'm clocking back in, and I got a patient that's been shot the hell up on my roster." I told her and she laughed. "For real girl. But come by later. I wanna see my grand babies." I told her and disconnected the call.

"Hey nurse Jackson. Would you be up to take room 7? Older guy just came in on a gunshot wound. It was through and through and he's stable and can leave maybe tomorrow." she told me giving details on the patient.

"Of course I can.... I have 7 more hours so I can." I told her and she smiled.

"Thanks Jack." she said calling me by my last name. I grabbed my papers I needed and headed around to the rooms. Going to the last room on the list, I heard laughter from the other side.

Knock, knock, knock.

"Come in." the lady voice yelled and I opened the door. I was shocked beyond words on what was on the other side of the door. The female stood when I entered the room. She was a pretty lady, maybe around my age or a tad bit older. She was skinny and light colored. I knew she was sitting on money because her fingers wrist and neck was dressed with jewelry. On her feet was some expensive shoes, and of course she had designer on. She wasn't why I was shocked though. The nigga laying in the bed was why.

"Jan?" Maseon said.

"Jesus. I guess karma caught up to yo ass." I hissed and started to check his vitals.

"How do y'all know each?" The lady started to say but Maseon cut her off.

"Give me a moment, Ahlana." he told her, and she looked at him like looks could kill.

"Give you a moment? What do y'all have to discuss in private?" she asked and I laughed.

"Girl, don't nobody want this no good ass nigga but you! Get out." I said, and she stood up.

"You are a nurse! You're not gonna talk to me like that." She shrieked and I sighed.

"Get out Ahlana." he told her firmly, and she took her ass on out.

"So how is my kids?" he asked once we were alone.

"I didn't know you had kids.... Shit last time I checked I raised my kids by myself, and did a great ass job doing so." I said after checking his blood pressure and giving him the medicine the doctor prescribed.

"You acting like I had a fucking choice! You gave me an ultimatum... Either my wife or you!" he said sitting up.

"No motherfucker! I gave you a choice, YOUR wife or your children! I told you to tell her about them or don't come back! You never came back, and I didn't chase yo ass!" I yelled feeling myself get worked up.

"Janet, it's not like that." He tried to reason but I put my hand up.

"It's exactly like that Mace. I knew you was married when I first started fucking you! I knew you weren't leaving yo wife for me! But you said if I had the kids you wasn't gone hide them and take care of them! You the one said, you was gone do right by the kids! I told you I didn't want them. I told you I wasn't ready!" I yelled and he grabbed for my hand.

"No, don't fucking touch me nigga! Don't you dare put the blame on me. I have been fine for fourteen years. I been okay alone again for fourteen years. Fuck you!" I yelled and started to leave but turned around...

"I have a fourteen-year-old son.... He's yours sorry motherfucker!" I hissed and walked out.

24

EVA

"Sit ya motherfucking ass down somewhere now! " I yelled at Braylon.

"Why can't she be like you Brit?" I joked and she smiled.

"Ain't nobody like me maw. I'm one of a kind," she said and I laughed.

"That's my girl."

Ring, ring, ring.

"Hello," I answer.

"What are you doing?" My sister Brenda asked me. I was the oldest of three; it was me, then my brother Erick, and our youngest sister Brenda. Brenda was Brandon's momma and me and her was real close!

"Nothing, babysitting your bad ass grandkids! They driving me wild!" I snapped.

"Sit yo ass down! Matter of fact, come on y'all. Y'all finna take a nap!" I yelled at Braylon as she skated through the house. I have been yelling and fussing at her ass all day long! If it ain't these damn kids of mine it was they children that was gone kill me!

"Sorry na-na." Brit apologized and I sighed.

"It's okay, come on!" I grabbed a cover from the closet and laid them on the couch. Bray at one end and Brit at the other.

"Get up and that's ya ass!" I yelled over my shoulder as I went to the front room to clean up.

"My bad sis. How are you doing?" I asked and she laughed.

"It's all good. I been good. They said I might be home earlier than I thought!" she said sounding cheerful. Brenda was locked up for drug trafficking and dealing with a lot of other charges. She had been locked up for about twenty-three years now. Brandon was just a baby when she went in and since then I took him in. Bran was my baby though.

"That's great sis! I have been trying to get yo knuckle headed ass son to bring these bad ass babies to see you!" I told her and she sighed.

"Brandon is...... Brandon is, stubborn. I'mma say, I don't want to say the wrong word. I know he still is mad at me because I wasn't there for him. He doesn't understand how much I regret it!" Brenda said and I sighed.

"It's gonna be okay sis! We gone make sure you get out of there and you get to see these babies grow up! We gone make sure these ones count!" I told her and I could hear her smile through the phone.

"I love you E!" She said and I laughed.

"I love you too sis! Anyways, so do you see Jameson?" I asked and she laughed.

"Girl yes. I see that half dead motherfucker every single day!" She sassed. "Why? Why you worried about that nigga anyways?" Brenda wondered.

"Sis! Don't start." I warned and she smacked her lips.

"Girl you don't start. Ever since you found out his dead

beat ass been working here you been coming more and answering more calls all that. What's up?" She asked and I sighed.

Brenda was right. Just like most men, Jamar and Tiera dad left me after I had Tiera. Jamar was an accident; he came back a year after I had Tiera, told me stories on how he wanted his family back and what not. Fucked me good and left me again! This time when I had Jamar he tried to come back years later, and I didn't fall for it. Fool me once shame on you, fool me twice shame on me, and it definitely won't be a third time!

"Look, I know how you feel about James. You can act hard all you want but I know the real you. James is married now and even though he asks about you and the kids all the time, he doesn't give a fuck about y'all. Just like Thomas don't give a fuck about Brandon and I. It's just what it is!" Brenda preached and I listened. It was an awkward silence for a second until I sighed.

"Thanks sis!" I told her and she laughed.

"You welcome. Now tell me all about my bad ass grand babies and what the fuck Bran been doing?" Brenda asked, and we chopped it up for about 20 more minutes. I promised I would get Bran to talk to her and bring the babies to see her. We disconnected the call.

After cleaning up my house, I started on my dinner. Kris came and got the kids and I could have sworn I saw a pudge. I ain't speak on it yet, because the truth will come out. I know facts; if one was pregnant then all was, because these women around me stayed pregnant at the same time!

Knock, Knock, Knock.

Walking to my front door, I made sure my big boy Beretta was on my hip. With all the shit my sons and nephews has going I had to stay strapped. I smiled and opened the door for Janet. Since Brenda been gone, I have always been a loner! So over the years, Janet and I became so close. That's my sister for life. Even if our kids were to ever go they separate ways, we was gone remain solid!

"Girl who here?" Janet asked looking around.

"Nobody. Your bad ass grandchildren just left!" I said rolling my eyes. "Girl they got on my nerves, but I love my babies! Okay, so what's up?" I wondered as I poured both of us a glass of wine.

"Girl I need something stronger than that." Janet sighed and walked to the den to take her shoes and coat off I'm guessing.

"I got what you need sister." I sang getting up. I turned the music on low and went to my stash. I pulled out the bottle of Courvoisier and the bag of the finest home grown weed ever courtesy of my son.

"Yes exactly what I need." she said grabbing a shot glass out the cabinet, pouring a shot and taking it.

"So let me tell you." she said smiling as I rolled a cigarillo. "Okay, so my day was fine. I got my daughters back talking, and you know with everything going on a bitch been real stressed the fuck out. Boom, so I gets a new patient, shot the fuck up. Why the fuck was it Mace and Mason daddy." She said slamming the shot glass down.

"This fucker got the nerve to ask me how his kids? KIDS... kids? I ain't know the nigga had fucking kids." she said. I knew she was upset because her hands were shaking and her eyes got watery.

"I told him about Chubby," she told me and I shook my head.

"I hope you ready for those skeletons to come out." I told her and she sighed.

"He need to know we have another son together!" she tried to reason but I shook my head.

"Okay, and what is that nigga gone do? Walk away a third time!" I said.

"Okay heffa. I know I fucked up. He just had me in a different head space." she said taking a long pull from the blunt in return making her cough.

"Take it easy homes.... take it easy." I said, and we both started laughing.

"So what you gonna do?" I wondered.

"I'm not gone do shit! His wife didn't know me so I'm pretty sure she doesn't know he has kids. I'mma let it be." I nodded agreeing. "Girl, that's just too much. Brought back old feelings that I tried so hard to bury. I'm not ready for that type of drama." she vented and I sighed.

"Girl don't!! Just steer far away from him. I'm telling you this is gonna be shit." I told her taking a sip of my drink. If it wasn't drama with the kids, it was drama somewhere else. I tell you this family gone stress me into an early grave.

25

CHARLES

I took a swig of the bottle and tossed it out the window. I didn't even drink like that, but lately, I drink to numb the pain. I was hurting lately and didn't know how to fix the pain.

I hit a U-turn and pulled into the alley. Turning my lights off and turning the ignition off, I made sure my hat was pulled low. I mean, it was four in the morning, so I'm pretty sure nobody even saw me coming. Walking up to the back door of the target house, I pulled my pocket knife and pushed it into the lock as hard as I could. I jiggled it twice then the door popped open. I smiled and rubbed my hands together; this was gone be so easy. I slowly tiptoed up the stairs as I screwed my silencer on. I stopped at the first room and peaked in. I saw a bunk bed with two kids in it. The upper level held three bedrooms and both rooms was occupied by children. I silently, prayed for forgiveness and shot each kid in the head. God know my heart and he know my heart is pure. The kids was better off dead than to live in this fucked up world.

Going to the last room, Lance and Morrisa laid in the

bed sleep like babies. I laughed and shot Morrisa in the head. As the bullet hit her head Lance jumped up. I silenced him with a bullet to his head also. I kissed his lips and stuck my knife right into his heart. Before I left out the same way I came in, I made sure the house was in untamable flames! Bout time the fire department comes those bodies was gone be burned to a crisp! Fuck them!

∼

"What I tell you about leaving there so late. Nobody there with you?" Karter voiced as I cleaned up my shop. It was going on midnight, and I finished my last client about fifteen minutes ago and was just now finishing cleaning up.

"Girl shit. I needed to make money. I'm trying to stay away from the illegal shit!" I told her. With everything going on with all this other shit, I was going through it. I thought taking Lance out was gone make me feel better but it didn't! All I thought about was killing him again. Lance was really the only one I gave my heart to and no matter how much I play hard, the shit was getting to me! I can't stop hearing them tell me that they were hired to kill me. Even after death this nigga was still hurting me some way!

"Man, that shit was hurtful." I said.

"You okay love? I know ever since that shit with Lance you been kind of, reckless. Not so much as reckless, but just careless." Karter said, and I put her on speaker phone as I gathered my bags. I slipped the phone into my pocket.

"I know. It's just it gets to me sometimes. Like damn I let my guard completely down thinking this nigga was all about me and whole time the nigga was plotting. Like I had this nigga around the kids, around the family, and around all of us! It's been times when that nigga could've got us together and, I wouldn't even see the shit coming!" I said. I was happy that I got them before they got me! When I turned all the lights out, I locked up the store and headed to my car.

"Girl, this fucking tattoo itch. You know I was in my feelings. Who the hell gets tattooed on they fingers." I said and we both laughed.

"Yeah bitch, you know you been on one lately! Can't nobody tell you shit!" Karter relied back...

I threw my bags in the passenger seat and hopped straight in. When I reached to push the button to start my car up, I felt somebody grab me by the neck and wrap a bag over my head.

"Night-night, nigga; go night-night," the voice kept saying but I kept swinging, scratching at the hands and bag. I felt my body giving up but instead I reached for my gun I kept on my side and started firing. The hands let go of me and I pulled the bag off gasping for air.

"What was that? Ci you cool? Ci?" Karter screamed through the phone. I heard shuffling around in her background as I caught my breath.

"I'm at the shop somebody just tried to..." before I could even finish I was knocked out cold by a gun crashing to my head.

26

KARTER

"Hey Marcel, have either one of you talked to Jamar, Little, or shit, Brandon?" I asked, slipping on my pants and sneakers.

"Nope.... I haven't." he said and I instantly got mad.

"I think something is wrong with Charles. Get a crew to the shop now." I said then hung up. Dialing Jamar again, this time it went to voicemail.

"Fuck!" I yelled and called Jania since she was the closest to me. She didn't answer either.

"Fuck," I groaned and dialed Kris... she was literally up the street but we was beefing right now so I didn't wanna call this bitch for shit! She answered on the first ring.

"Sis, can you get to my house like now?" I asked soon as she said hello.

"Yeah... yeah, what's wrong?" she asked.

"Just please get here now. The kids sleep. Use the key... I gotta go check on Charles." I told her and she said she'll be here in five minutes. I grabbed my purse and keys and made sure my pistol Jamar had got me a few months back was on my side. I hopped into Jamar's bulletproof Audi A6. I backed out the garage as Kris was pulling in. I hit her with a head nod and did the dash to Charles' shop. When I got there, yellow tape was out there and police cars. I hit the steering wheel and hopped out. It was a body bag on the ground next to Charles' car, and I instantly started to cry thinking the worst.

"Hey, excuse me... Who is that?" I asked the police man that walked past. He ignored me and kept going. "Excuse me. Tell me something! This is my brother's shop! That's my brother's car!" I yelled but they kept going. *Fuck*!

I dialed Jamar's phone, and it went to voicemail, then I tried Little and Brandon. I tried Eva and she didn't answer so I tried Tiera and Jania. It seem like it was fuck Karter tonight cause I couldn't get a hold of nobody right now. I saw the police captain that Jamar kept on the payroll coming my way.

"Hey, what's up Karter?" Antwon spoke.

"Ant. Is that Charles?" I asked and he sighed.

"I'm not sure who it is right now. They face is……. listen the face was detached . Is that Charles' car?" he asked, and I nodded with tears streaming down my face.

"Hey, where is Jock and the crew?" He whispered the last part.

"I can't get in touch with them. I can't get in touch with nobody." I sighed and wiped my face. When they picked the body up from the ground, the leg fell out and I saw the shoes. A little bit of my worries went out the window because the shoes wasn't Charles' shoes.

"That's not Charles! That's not Charles' shoes! C feet not that big Ant." I slowly said and he looked backwards.

"Let me go take a look." he said and walked away. He went to talk to the crime scene people and went back to the body then examined the car. After looking for, I guess, clues for a while he came back.

"Yeah, that wasn't Charles.... That was a known Jamaican cat that we been trying to get in our custody for human trafficking for a while..." he went through his phone and showed me a picture.

"His name is Jaden Linslow. Originally from Negril, Jamaica." he said and showed me a picture of a dude.

"Marlo?" I asked and he sighed.

"Yeah, his brother is Marlon. Missing guy report was filed for Marlon. That's what brought Jaden here. Listen, I don't know what business they have with the Haitians but...... Follow me." he sighed and we walked to his car. He handed me a folder and told me to give it to Jamar. I nodded and went back to my car. I dialed Charles' phone, and it rung and went to voicemail. I pulled up the *Find My Friend* app and clicked on Charles' name. His phone was 25 minutes from where I was so I headed that way. When I got to a secluded area, I grabbed both my guns and set them on my lap. I pulled over when I reached my destination, but it was nothing but grass and cornfield. I called Charles phone and looked around but couldn't see nothing. I got out the car and stood looking around. It wasn't shit out here! His phone location was turned off. I dialed his number again and it went straight to voicemail.

"FUCK!" I hissed and turned back around. I dialed Jamar phone on the way back home.... still went to voicemail.

～

"I DON'T KNOW. Listen, all I know is we was on the phone. I

heard struggling or something. I don't know.... fuck." I yelled out still pacing the floor.

"Karter man, what you mean you don't know?" Jamar hissed in my face.

"Bro, back up." Little said getting in between us but I didn't back down! The way I was feeling this morning I wanted all smoke with whoEVER.

"Listen y'all. Brandon and Little!" I specifically said mugging Jamar.

"We were on the phone, and he was telling me about how he was still fucked up about Lance. I heard struggling or something, maybe. I don't know; then I heard shots. And heard Charles breathing, and he said he was at the shop and somebody was trying to get him, but before he finished what he was saying, I heard a cracking sound and it went silent." I looked at Jamar and my tears finally fell.

"I kept calling you and kept calling. Nobody answered. I went to the shops because I knew he was leaving there...... I saw Ant and he said the dude that was dead there was Marlon's brother from Jamaican." I said and sat down.

"I just told him he shouldn't be at the shop late like that with all the shit going on." I voiced and Jamar looked at me with pure disgust.

"Listen, we're gonna find him. I promise that! Charles ain't no weak nigga, and he ain't going out without a fight period!" Eva voiced, and Kris walked in with all the kids following behind her.

"Mommy." KJ yelled and ran to me. All the other kids followed right after me when they noticed I was standing there. I hugged my babies.

"I was looking for you this morning. Where were you?" Ashtyn said with her hands on her hips.

"Yo daddy right there." I pointed to Jamar, and she turned around and looked at him then turned back to me.

"Oh, hey dad." she waved and then turned to me.

"I think you shouldn't leave without seeing us first. We were worried!" Ashtyn said and I laughed.

"I love you, too, Ash. Now go play with yo brothers and sisters." I kissed her forehead and she skipped off.

"Listen, with everything going on, I just feel like these niggas had something to do with Charles being gone! So call Mace and see if he can check all local police stations, hospitals, and everything. Morgues, all that." Jamar spoke and two of his dudes nodded and walked away.

"From now on, nobody go nowhere without protection! Make sure y'all got men with y'all at all time! And double security around the kids." Jamar spoke and I sighed. I went to the back and checked on the kids for a second then I went to the front room where Kris was sitting with Jania.

"Sis, thank you." I said hugging Kris.

"Girl, you know it's all love." she said and I smiled.

"Ain't nobody called Tiera?" Jania asked rolling her eyes.

"Nope. She don't fuck with me." I shrugged and Kris nodded.

"She's on some weird shit. She been calling my phone playing on my shit and everything talking about she gone kill me. She's crazy!" Jania laughed and I shook my head.

"It's just too much shit going on. What the hell!" I pouted feeling myself getting emotional again. Jamar stood at the doorway and cleared his throat.

"Can I holler at you for a second?" he asked, and I shrugged and followed him to the bathroom down the hallway. We both entered and he closed the door.

"Look, I'm leaving for about two days. We gone be in the streets trying to see what we can find on C. I need you and the girls to get the kids to mama's and hold shit down. Can you handle that simple task?" he asked and I nodded. "Are you sure? Cause right now I'm feeling like I can't even leave the house. Every time I look up it's something." He said. We just looked at each other.

"Okay, so what you saying it's my fault?" I asked, and Jamar didn't say nothing. "You know what.... I'mma just gone head and leave before I say...... Like, it's really fucked up that you feel like that but I'm the one that hit the dash across the city to get to the shop! I'm the one that cruised the city all night looking for anything! Fuck you Jamar! I break my fucking back day and night and you say it's my fault.... it's my fault cause they after us? It's my fault cause Charles missing!" I screamed and he looked at me.

"I shouldn't have even been fucking with you. All this wouldn't have happened. Now my brother missing man! My nigga missing, my house and shit getting shot at. Shit just not making sense." he yelled stepping into my face.

"And all this is my fault? " I asked feeling the tears roll down my face.

"Look, I don't think this shit is working out anyways. We fight too much and I don't even wanna come home sometimes to argue with you." Jamar said and I laughed.

"You know what, I'mma just gone ahead and leave now... Because you got me so fucked up right now yo. Cause you really got me fucked up." I said and grabbed the door knob.

"You can stay at the crib. I'll just get some of my stuff and move to ma dukes or something until I find something else." Jamar called after me and all my train of thought went left. I couldn't control myself as I swung and connected with his face. I didn't stop. I still swung even after he threw me to the wall and had me pinned up. I still was swinging. My fist wasn't no match for him; that nigga was at least two whole feet taller and at least a hundred something pounds heavier. I ain't give a fuck. I kept swinging until I felt my legs rise off the floor.

"Fuck you Jamar! You ain't shit nigga!" I yelled, tears flowing steady trying to swing!

"Chill the fuck out man." Jamar roared and pushed me against the wall with a little more force. "I'm done shorty. This ain't it!" he said and walked out of the bathroom.

27

TEIRA

I laughed as I watched as Jania walked out my momma front door. She hopped into her car and drove off, and I followed her. I knew she wasn't going nowhere far without Little sniffing under her ass. The nigga I paid to get rid of her failed miserably and from the way Little and Jamar had been blowing my phone up, he most likely told. Oh well, it wouldn't be the first time I killed one of Tyree bitches, and I'm pretty sure she won't be the last. Besides, Jamar was my brother. He was riding with me regardless.

When she pulled up into her house complex, I got excited, because I knew this was my time. She parked, and I hopped out my car. I ran up on her and shoved her with my gun.

"Hurry up and unlock the door bitch." I hissed pushing her.

"This gotta be a joke." she said and unlocked the door. Soon as it opened up, I pushed her inside and she turned around shaking her head.

"Teira..." she tried to say but I slapped the shit out of her.

"I tried to give you a choice to leave him alone and go on with yo little life but you just won't take the hint!" I roared and slapped her again. I had my gun pointed at her stomach and she looked from the gun to my face.

"Listen..."

"Shut the fuck up!" I yelled and tried to slap her again but she caught my hand and pushed me backwards. I still had my gun pointed at her.

"Come on now, Tiera; it's not that deep! If you want me gone then I'll leave! Shit, I ain't trying die over no nigga!" she reasoned and I laughed.

"Too late bitch! I been told you to beat it. Now you gotta die." I yelled and cocked my gun.

"How can you be worried about me when Charles is fucking missing!" she yelled and that caught me off guard.

"What you mean Charles missing?" I asked putting my gun down, and she charged at me knocking the gun out my hand making me fall backwards. The impact from the fall knocked the wind out of me, and she got on top of me. We both started swinging but my hits wasn't connecting. I had some hands to be small but with this big ass belly on me I couldn't swing how I wanted to. Her hits kept going and mine was slowing down.

"Bitch, don't you ever pull a gun on me ever!" She yelled in between punches. I reached for my gun that fell on the side of us but it was further away.

"Get the fuck off me bitch! I'm fucking pregnant!" I yelled but she ain't stop swinging. Tiera reached for the gun and we both grabbed it at the same time!

"Let it go bitch." She yelled and cracked me in the face. I didn't even have the energy to fight no more, but when she held the gun up to me I launched for it and we started tussling with it.

Pow!

My eyes shot up and I fell backwards. Jania fell backwards next to me and the last thing I saw was her eyes looking back at me before my eyes closed.

28

JAMAR

"Jamar! Jamar!" Karter screamed and cried for me but I kept walking, leaving her in the bathroom. I stopped for a second regretting how I just handled her but then Charles flashed through my mind.

"FUCK!" I hissed and kept walking to the front room where my family was.

"Let me say bye to my kids then..."

Knock, knock, knock.

Everybody got silent and reached for they pistol. I saw out the corner of my eyes Karter walking into the front room with the kids behind her. Her eyes still had tears in them but she wiped them quickly and grabbed her purse.

Knock, knock, knock.

Grabbing my pistol out my pants I peeked through the peephole.

"It's the mailman." I said and looked at my mama. She nodded and I opened the door. He had a package in his hand and a clipboard. It wasn't nothing fishy but I was still on alert.

"Open it." I stated calmly and he looked at me.

"Look bra, we didn't order shit! We don't take suspicious packages and shit so open it.... Before I blow yo fucking brains out." I said raising my gun aiming it at his head.

"Alright man, Alright man!" he set the box down and took a key and slid it down the middle. He opened it and it was gift paper on the top; he looked at me and then at my family right behind me looking down at the package.

"Go head and take that paper out." I ordered and he shook his head.

"Come on man. What..." he started to say.

"What the fuck did I just say nigga?" I roared pushing my strap into his temple. He pulled the paper back slowly.

"What the fuck." he whispered and turned around throwing up. I picked the package up to get a better look and felt sick to my stomach.

"Oh my god." Karter cried and I dropped the package.

"Get in the house.... Get the fuck in the house." I yelled grabbing the note that was attached to the package.

"Every week somebody in your family gone come up missing, get sent back to you piece by piece until you're the last standing. Start planning Funerals." It read. I looked at Karter and she was silently crying while hugging the kids in her arms.

Knock, knock, knock!

"Fuck!" I yelled and Little pulled his strap out going towards the door. He peeked out and slipped his gun in the back of his pants.

"It's Ant." he said and opened the door.

"I been calling y'all man.... We got a problem. We found a body this morning. I'm pretty sure this finger was the missing part." he voiced holding up Charles finger that was just delivered to us.

. . .

TO BE CONTINUED.........

SUBSCRIBE

Text Shan to 22828 to stay up to date with new releases, sneak peeks, contest, and more....